DIGITAL BLADE

The Cursed Blade Series

M.P. Starkweather

Phoenix Eclipse Publishing

I want to dedicate this book to my two biggest fans, my husband Josh and my son Thom, who will probably never read any of my books. Thanks for pushing me to chase my dream. I love you both to the moon and back.

Author's Note

This book was previously published as *Taking It Off*, and was part of a different series. I hope that you will give this new series a chance. There are a few changes and additions to start off The Cursed Blade Series, and I'm excited to see this idea take flight.

Please be aware of content warnings for this story. There are graphic descriptions of murder for hire, flashbacks of child abuse, sexual abuse and human trafficking, graphic language and sexual situations involving multiple partners at once. There are unique shifters, who have abilities that are used during intimate times.

Your mental health is important, so please be aware of the content warnings as you begin.

Acknowledgments

I would like to thank:

My author besties, who encourage me to keep writing, even when it's hard;

My amazing PA, Gwen, who is my twinsie;

My Alpha Team who tries hard to keep me on track;

My Editing Team who does their best to make sure my books make sense and have as few typos as possible;

My Cover Artist, Wallflower Designs, who's responsible for the gorgeous images on the front of this book

and My ARC Team, who catch some of the things the rest of us miss.

CONTENTS

CAMGIRL ASSASSIN

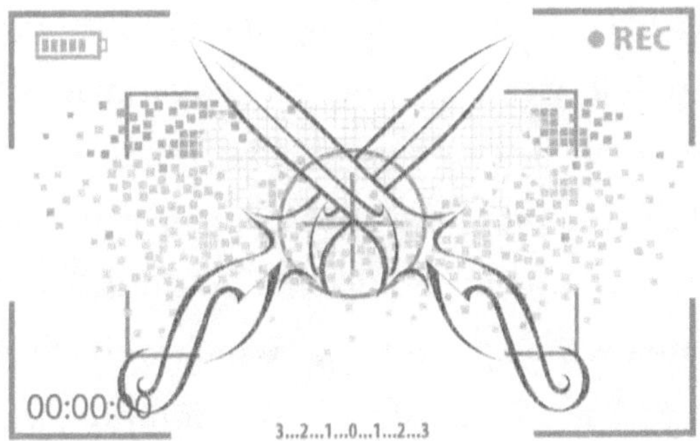

EMILY

After securing my purple masquerade mask, I tug my dark green wig into place. I'm not rushing, even though I took longer than I should to get ready. This has to go just right. I only have one shot to get what I need. I know what Davis likes, but I have to find out what he's planning. The only way to do that is to get into his computer.

And to get into his system, I need a link. A smirk crosses my face as I switch on the cam while I settle on the bed. I know I won't have long to wait, and I need to get into character before he logs on. Jasmin isn't shy. She enjoys showing her body to men in exchange for money. I have to admit, part of me does too. It's what allows me to use this as my cover; to become Jasmin when I need to. Well, that, and I may be a bit of a voyeur. I like being watched.

I glance around the simple room, making sure everything is in place. The hidden cams I have set up throughout the apartment are virtually invisible. The walls are a soft white, to give the impression that I'm more innocent than I am.

A rack full of wigs in almost every color imaginable covers one wall, next to the closet that holds my costumes; each one color coordinated with the wigs. I call them costumes, because I don't think a woman should have to dress like this to get attention unless she's performing. Which is exactly what I do. I put on my mask and transform from Emily to Jasmin.

Everything in this room is designed to help me pull off the con. And the con is designed to make it easier to kill. It really shouldn't be so easy for me to take a life. I do have moral standards, though. I won't kill an innocent, and I always check out my marks beforehand so I know what I'm dealing with. Most get two or three cam calls so I can gather enough information to make the decision.

So far, none of them have been innocent. My favorite kills are the ones related to the sex trafficking ring that the cops can't seem to pin down. It's funny how working outside the law gives me an advantage to enforcing it. Sometimes I wonder if that makes me worse than the men I take out.

I shrug, willing to accept that I'm a monster who hunts other monsters. The fact that I get paid for it is icing on the cake.

While appearing to be relaxed and waiting for Davis to join our video chat, I double and triple check my connections. Then I tap into my phone and make sure it's on silent. Sometimes I amaze myself at my ability to multi-task this way. It's all part of my digital shifter ability. I'm always connected to my system and can control it with nothing more than a thought.

It's always felt strange, being human and somehow digital at the same time. I'm not sure what kind of magic my mother held, but I know my abilities came from her.

Since my pixelated form can't be caught on camera, I get away with everything. It doesn't matter if I'm accessing a bank account to drain it, hacking a computer for blackmail purposes, or even committing murder for money. No one has ever figured out that I am Umbr4g3_R0gu3 (Umbrage Rogue) because of my unique shifter power. Digital shifters are rare, and we tend to hide our abilities. I'm not saying most people who can do what I can are criminals, but I'm not *not* saying it either.

I'm distracted from my thoughts by the soft chime letting me know that Davis is entering the video chat. With an inward sigh, I put on my sweet smile and prepare to multi-task.

"Good evening, sweet Jasmin. I've been looking forward to this all day," he says the moment he can see me.

"I've missed you," I coo, knowing that he's about to give me the chance I need to find a way into his computer. "How was your day?"

I pretend to listen as he drones on about his day and how difficult it is to run a world-wide conglomerate, all while jerking off while he stares at me. He's done this a couple of times before, and I resist the urge to roll my eyes a few times. His story is boring and self-centered, but somehow telling me about his company dealings gets him off. Maybe it's because I'm watching him masturbate, I don't know.

Just as he finishes, both his story and shooting his load, my pixelated tendrils find the spot I've been searching for. I have my way in. A quick time check tells me we only have about two minutes left of our allotted time. Hmm, it took him longer today than usual. I'm relieved that he seems satisfied with just unloading on me today, and not as interested in crafting a story for me to act out.

Some of his 'interests' are beyond Emily's comfort zone. That's part of the reason I become Jasmin for this part of my work. He's an attractive older man, but after learning about his hidden agenda, I find him much less appealing. Especially when he wants to watch me fuck random household items.

"I'm sorry, Davis, but our time is up for today. You'll have to book another chat for next week," I say, cutting our time short by a minute. It's easy to make the offer for another video call when I know he'll be dead in less than twelve hours. The smile on my face is genuine for once, and I hope he doesn't notice the difference.

"Oh, well, damn. I thought we had longer," he argues. "Can't we just extend the appointment? I'll pay triple."

I force myself to appear as if I'm considering his offer, then I shake my head. "Unfortunately, I have other clients to see today, and I can't reschedule." He nods his understanding and thanks me for my time. I disconnect the call and verify the transfer of funds went through. It's messier if I have to take his money before I kill him. Much easier for everyone if he pays like he's supposed to. The payments are routed through the dark web and will be impossible to trace.

When I'm sure the money has transferred, I move it to my hidden account, then shut my system down manually. Even though I can't be traced, I won't use my cam set up for my other job. I have a separate system for that. I walk around the room, switching off the ring lights, before heading to the wall where a hidden panel opens. Walking through, I reach out to the computer inside the small room and turn it on, then secure the door.

If anyone were to come into my apartment right now, they'd think I wasn't home. And that's exactly what I want them to think. I don't expect the guys to come over, but I have to be careful anyway. I've never invited them into my apartment, because I don't want them to discover any of my secrets—digital shifter, cam girl, assassin.

A quick check of the time tells me that I need to get moving or I'll be late. I do have dinner plans, after all. Then I have to come back and take care of Davis. But first, I must collect the evidence my benefactor wants on the sex trafficking ring that Davis is involved in. If I'm being honest, I'd probably offer my services for free just to be the one to off this guy. I do like the money, though.

Reaching out with my digital tendrils, I search Davis' computer. Oh, this man is a sicko. And not a smart one, either. He has pictures, names, dates—what kind of idiot saves this shit to his personal computer? I get needing insurance, but come on. At least put it on a private server or a USB drive or something. I wonder how he's kept this from his wife. Or does she know and keep his secret for him? I shudder at the thought.

Copying the files takes longer than I expected, and now I'm running late. The guys will come looking for me if I don't get over there soon. It's a good thing their apartment is just a couple of floors up from mine. I secure the files on a flash drive and encrypt it before dropping it into a padded envelope. Could I deliver these files electronically? Absolutely. Would it be easier than this cloak and dagger shit? Definitely. But there would be more of a chance that I'd out myself to the people who hire me. So, I'll stick with the plan.

I don't have time to run out and deliver the package right now, so it'll have to wait. They don't need it until after I finish Davis off anyway. I close my eyes for a moment and check my hidden cameras to make sure I'm still alone before I exit the secret room and change for dinner. There's no time for a shower, so I toss the wig onto the bed with my mask, and I wipe away as much of the heavy makeup as I can without making myself look homeless. I've lived in this building for years, and known my guys almost that long. I think about how our relationship started, and it makes me laugh. Each of them asked me out, and I said yes...then found out that they're roommates. Things could have gotten awkward, but they're more like brothers, so they decided to share. I was relieved that they didn't ask me to choose.

I shake away those thoughts and rush to change clothes. The leggings and sweatshirt are way more comfortable than the lacy bra and thong I have on underneath. I grab my keys and phone, then race up the stairs. I'm standing in front of their door when Jeremy opens it, presumably to come find me. He jumps when he almost runs into me.

"You're late. Luke was about to start eating without you. Will was going to call the cops. Of course, I knew you'd be here when you got here, so I wasn't worried," he teases. I laugh and push him out of the way so I can enter the much larger apartment.

"You three are impossible. I got caught up with work and lost track of time. Sorry," I try to avoid talking about work, because I'm not sure how they'd take the news if they knew what I do for a living. Either job, really. Most guys claim that they'd be okay dating a cam girl, but it always turns into accusations and jealousy. I'd rather avoid that if I can. Besides, what the four of us have is pretty casual. We mostly hang out, and occasionally fuck.

"Oh, that smells amazing! What did you make, Luke?" I ask as I enter the kitchen. It smells like an Italian restaurant in here, and I can't quite make out what dish it could be.

"Lasagna, salad, and tiramisu. I don't think you understand how hard it is to keep these two from starting without you," he jokes, kissing my cheek. I wrap my arms around him and squeeze.

"Well, let's not make them wait any longer," I say, dragging him toward the dining room. I swear this apartment is three times the size of mine. I have no idea how we're even in the same building. But I'm glad we are. Otherwise, I'd be eating take out way more than I do.

I help Luke take the food to the table and find Will setting the plates and silverware around. "It's about time you got here."

"Were you having trouble keeping the other two in line?" I ask, guessing that he's teasing me too.

"Nope. I just missed your face, that's all," he says before pulling me into his arms and kissing me hard. If I didn't know better, I would think we were a couple. But the four of us agreed to keep things casual, because they all want me, and I won't make a decision that would hurt any of them.

When he breaks the kiss, I can't help teasing him. "Kissing a girl like that will make her think you have ulterior motives."

Will winks at me, "What if I do?" My cheeks flush and I twist out of his arms. I practically run away any time one of them says anything that might take our arrangement to the level of relationship. There's no way I can balance dating the three of them with my other two lives. Is there?

During dinner, I try not to think about what I have to do later. I don't mind killing someone who deserves it; honestly, it gets me going. So maybe if I focus on that part of it, I can have some fun before I have to get dirty. Is it weird that murder turns me on?

"Why don't you just stay tonight?" Jeremy asks as Luke and Will clear the aftermath of dinner from the table. The offer is tempting, especially since I'd like to get them all naked, but I can't delay my job any longer. Gaining access to Davis' system took a week longer than it should have. There's no telling how many women are suffering because of that delay.

"I can't. I have to work later," I say, not thinking that one of them will question me about my job. I'm usually very careful not to mention work because I don't like answering their inquiries. *Fuck.* Realization dawns just as a smirk crosses Jeremy's face.

"You know that you don't have to work if you don't want to. We'll take care of you. Between the three of us, we have plenty of money," he offers. It's sweet, but this is supposed to be casual, and that sounds more like commitment. I can't handle this conversation.

I slide from my chair and onto his lap. Wrapping my arms around his neck, I lean in and kiss him. Straddling him, I can feel exactly what the kiss does to him. My tongue strokes his as I grind against his growing cock. Hums of approval tell me the moment Will and Luke reenter the room. I don't let go of Jeremy or stop kissing him.

A moment later, I feel body heat on either side of me. I'm essentially boxed in, and I love it. I break the kiss and whisper, "Why don't we have some fun before I have to go?"

None of them respond, but I'm scooped up and carried to Will's room. He tosses me gently on the bed, laughing when I bounce. I can't help laughing with him until the look in his eyes sobers me. Will is suddenly serious and I'm not sure if I like it.

The three of them stand next to the bed, staring down at me. Before I can say anything, they've stripped down and are climbing in the bed with me. I look my fill, like I always do when they take this approach. I don't mind when they put me on display for them, either, but there's something special about being able to stare at their chiseled naked bodies while they stalk toward me.

Luke captures my lips with his while Jeremy drags my leggings off and tosses them aside. He breaks the kiss long enough for Will to pull my sweatshirt off and throw it wherever my leggings landed. I expect him to come back and kiss me more, but the three of them freeze and exchange a look.

"What? You're making me paranoid," I say, feeling insecure for the first time with them.

"Well, that explains the body glitter," Luke says with a chuckle.

"I'm definitely not mad at it," Jeremy responds.

"What are you talking about?" I ask, not understanding what's happening.

"Em, we know your secret," Will says with a smirk. Oh, fuck. How did they figure out that I'm a secret assassin?

"What? I don't have any secrets," I insist, hoping I can get them off my trail. How did these three figure me out when no one has been able to catch me in the past five years I've been doing this?

"Come on, Em," Jeremy says.

"It's okay, doll. We're not upset. If anything, it's a major turn on," Luke adds. Wait, what the fuck is he talking about? They get turned on by murder? So, I'm not the only one. Hmm...this could be interesting.

"We watched your live stream earlier, Jasmin," Will says. My eyes widen and I feel my cheeks heat. Oh. That secret. Okay, this isn't completely ruined.

"You're not weirded out by it? Some guys would be." I bite my lower lip and furrow my brow.

Jeremy licks his lips. "As long as we know you're saving that tight, wet, pussy for us, you can show it to whoever you want, Em." His words rattle through me and I'm even wetter than I was. I should be upset because his statement is a lot like giving me permission, but I'm too turned on to worry about that right now.

Will grabs my thong and peels it off me. "I can't wait any longer. I need to taste you. That stream was hot, and I've been waiting for you to come over all day." He buries his face in my mound, sniffing deeply before lapping his tongue along my slit.

Luke removes my bra next, and I realize exactly how they figured it out. I didn't change out of the lingerie I wore for the stream. Fuck. Well, at least they didn't learn my other secret. I just have to be more careful.

Jeremy and Luke move to either side of me while Will worships my center. I wrap a hand around each of their cocks and stroke, dragging them closer to my lips. I lick one, then the other, before I lose my ability to concentrate because Will flicks his tongue against my clit, sending me over the edge. I throw my head back and moan at the sensations that rip through me.

These guys don't give me time to recover, switching positions while I'm distracted. Jeremy grabs my hips and flips me on top of him, easing me down on his engorged member. A moment later, I feel Luke rubbing and kneading my ass cheeks before spreading me open and smearing lube on my rosebud. I gasp at the cold liquid, and Will captures my lips with his, giving me a taste of my release.

They all know my boundaries, and I'm not afraid to use my safe word if needed. But these three also know everything I enjoy, and they're determined to give it all to me tonight. I pull Will closer and guide his cock into my mouth as Luke eases himself into my ass. I want the three of them to use me for their pleasure.

Jeremy supports my weight while I maneuver Will into position so he can fuck my mouth in time with Jeremy and Luke. Six hands explore my body while these three cocks ease into a rhythm that will push away everything I've been preoccupied with today.

I let myself relax and they each pick up the pace; Jeremy and Will thrust into me while Luke pulls out, then they switch. Each cock thrusts into me over and over, until I cry out my release around Will's dick. The vibration sets off his release, and the other two follow a few short thrusts later.

When Will steps away to get a damp rag, I collapse on Jeremy. Luke eases out of me and drops onto the bed next to us, lying on his back. Will tosses him a rag, then proceeds to roll me off of Jeremy and clean me up. I love how attentive they are, taking care of me and showing me that they care. It's almost like a real relationship.

But we agreed to keep things casual, so I'm not letting myself go there. Besides, I really do have to work tonight. Is it wrong to let them think I'll be on cam instead of telling them it's not that kind of job? Maybe, but I'm not about to spill the beans about what I've actually got planned. A quick check of the time tells me I need to get moving.

"I have to go get ready for work. But I'll see you guys tomorrow, right?" I kiss each of them and throw my clothes on quickly. As soon as they confirm that we're on for tomorrow, I dash from their apartment, racing back to mine.

Davis' schedule is very strict, and I have a small window of opportunity if I want to do this tonight. Putting it off any longer isn't an option. I slip into my apartment, locking the door behind me. I have just enough time for a quick shower, just so I don't smell like sex when I materialize in Davis' house. I don't want him to have any warning for what's coming.

After my shower, I double check the lock on the front door, then head to my secret room. Once I'm locked inside, I let my body shift into my pixelated form. It's been a few days, and it feels good to change. Letting myself stretch, I check my text messages and emails.

As expected, I have a text from each of the guys. They've decided that we're going out tomorrow instead of staying in. I have three options to choose from for dinner and will need to choose once I'm finished working. The emails are all from my client checking in to make sure the job will be completed on schedule. Why they decided to send three emails to ask if I'm going to finish the job tonight is beyond me. I'll wait and respond to that after, when I have proof. I'm careful to disconnect from the dark web account where I get my jobs, then I focus on the task at hand.

How do I want to take Davis out? I could just reach in and crush his heart. That's effective, but not very satisfying. I could make it look like a suicide and leave a typed note about everything he's involved with. Or I can rip his head off and let his blood spray all over me. I guess I'll just decide in the moment. I know I can make it as painless or painful as I want. I love having the power to choose exactly how I take these men out. I can be as messy as I want or keep it clean and make it look like natural causes. Most of the time, I turn the monster loose and get things messy. It's not like anyone will know I was there anyway.

I slide into my computer, stretching and feeling my way through the connection I formed with Davis' system earlier. Shutting down his security system and cameras is easy, and in just a few moments, I'm standing next to his computer in what looks like a rich man's study. Leather-bound books fill the wall-to-wall bookshelves, and a mahogany desk sits in front of the window. His computer has the spot of honor on one side of the desk. Two overstuffed leather chairs face the desk, and I roll my eyes at how over-the-top the whole room is.

Closing my eyes, I listen for movement. According to his schedule, Davis should be alone for another twenty minutes. Then his wife and kids will return from dinner with her parents, and they'll find the aftermath of my work. Not hearing anything, I tap into his cell phone, and discover that he's watching porn. Well, that makes this easier.

I find him in the bedroom across the hall, which appears to be the master suite. He's sitting in a chair with his back to me and streaming the obviously homemade porn on the large television in the corner. Tears stream down the young woman's face as a man fucks her ass while another stands in front of her stroking his cock. I hold back a growl as he rams his dick into her mouth. It's possible that this is completely consensual, but it doesn't appear that way.

Is this what they're forcing the kidnapped women to do? The thought repulses me and fills me with rage. This man will pay, with his life and his reputation.

It takes less than a minute to cross the room in my pixelated form. I stand behind Davis and place my hands on either side of his head. He tries to turn to see who's here, but I twist and pull his head, tearing it from his shoulders and showering myself in his blood.

Dropping the severed head onto the floor, I disappear into his abandoned cell phone.

A STRANGE INVITATION

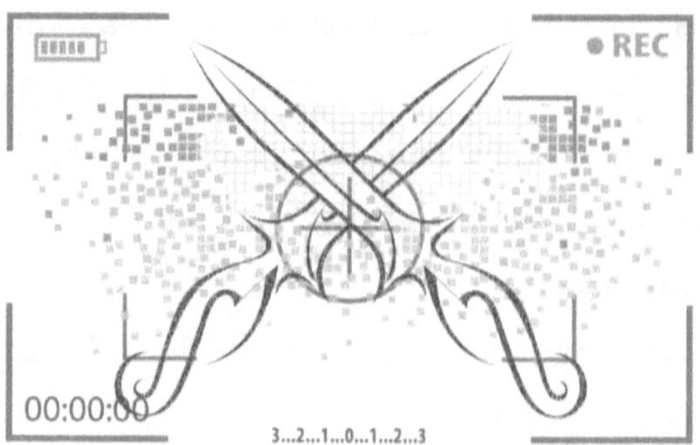

EMILY

After delivering the proof of both Davis' involvement in the sex trafficking ring, and his untimely demise, to the bus station locker as agreed upon, I head home and collapse on the bed. I had to shower before I could leave the apartment to do the drop, so I don't have to worry about ruining my sheets now.

I glance at the clock and chuckle. Twelve minutes after midnight. That's not bad for everything I've managed to accomplish since I left the guys' apartment. Something leaning against my clock catches my attention. Is that a piece of paper?

As much as I want to ignore it and sleep, I feel drawn to whatever it is. I must know. It can't wait.

I drag myself out of bed and stumble across the room. Why is my alarm clock so far away? Oh, yeah. Because I'll turn it off in my sleep if it's closer. Of course, I can still turn it off when it's across the room by using my powers, but I guess whatever works to trick my mind into not ignoring the damned thing. A small hot pink envelope is propped up against the back of my clock. How did that get there?

I look around the room, confused. I know I locked the door and set the security system when I left. There's no way someone could get inside without me knowing. I have the most state-of-the-art security system that exists. Turning the envelope over in my hands, I slink back to bed. I'll read this and sleep, then I'll figure out what's wrong with my security. If someone wanted to kill me, they already could have. Somehow that thought is less comforting than I want it to be. A quick check of the system can't hurt.

I tap into the system and see that nothing is amiss. It seems to be working fine. I'll run a full diagnostic on it later to be sure, but for now, I think everything is okay. Besides the mystery note, that is. And the fact that someone got into my apartment without triggering my alarm. I'll worry about that tomorrow. I'm too wiped to deal with it right now.

There's no writing on the outside of the envelope, and it's not sealed. I ease it open, wondering if it's filled with some sort of poison, or if it'll explode. When nothing poofs out at me, I look inside, and find a single sheet of matching hot pink paper. Upon opening it, I see glowing white letters adorning the dark sheet.

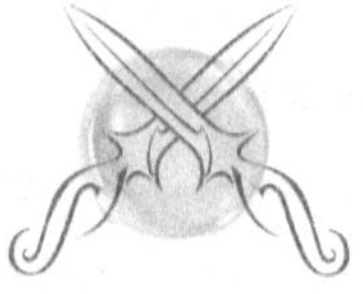

Emily,

You have been selected for an opportunity to audition to join the Cursed Blade.

If recruited, you will be provided targets that align with your moral compass. You will be given access to unlimited funding and equipment. You will also have the opportunity to recruit your own support team.

If interested, be at the docks in exactly twenty-four hours. Come alone. This is a one-time opportunity, and will not be offered again. We appreciate your discretion in this matter.

We hope to see you soon.

~B

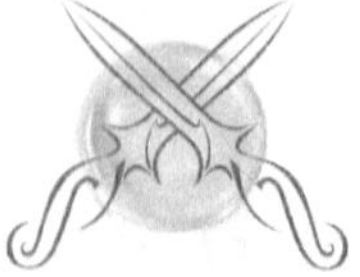

I read the glowing words over and over. Of course, there are rumors in my dark web circles of a guild of assassins, but I never expected to receive an invitation for an audition. This seems almost too good to be true. They guarantee that no mark will be against my moral code. And I'll have access to more money than I'll ever be able to spend. Why would they choose me? How did they even find me?

But it also means I'll never have a normal life. Would I have one if I don't accept? I don't know. I have twenty-four hours to consider the offer. If they really know everything, then they'll know the exact moment I read this. I glance at the clock again. That means I have until a quarter after midnight tomorrow to decide. How do I even go about making this big of a decision?

If I do this, I'll have to be at the docks at a quarter after midnight tomorrow. I need sleep, then I'll be able to give this decision the attention it deserves. I slip the paper back into the envelope and put it in the drawer beside my bed. No one ever comes here, but I want to protect it anyway. Especially if someone broke into my home to deliver this. There's no way to know if they'll come back.

I can't keep my eyes open any longer, sinking back into the soft mattress and dragging the covers over me. With images of money and danger dancing in my head, I drift off to sleep.

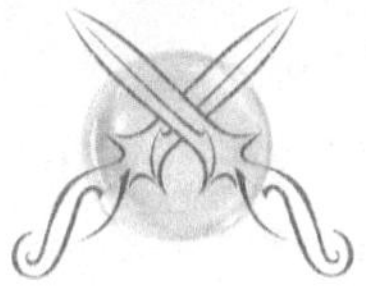

I wake early, the weight of my decision looming over my head. I was so proud of myself for what I did last night, but now I'm feeling melancholic. I'm still proud, but now I can't chase the worry from my mind. I don't feel guilty for killing Davis, but I am a little sad about taking a life. I guess that means I'm not a complete monster. There is no way to make a major life decision while I'm in this state. I can't clear my mind enough, and I don't want to make this big of a decision on impulse. I need something to distract me.

I know that Luke won't be up yet, because my vampire boy always sleeps in. A quick check of the time tells me it's even too early for my favorite wolf shifter, Jeremy. Which leaves Will, my insomniac shapeshifter. There's a chance he's up already, but I don't want to bother him if he's not. Sometimes I feel like I relate more to him because we're both rare shifters. He doesn't know that, but maybe someday I'll be able to share. So far, I've hidden my powers from them. I'm worried that they'll see me as a monster if they learn my secrets.

Using my powers, I tap into my phone and check social media. The moment my status changes to online, Will hops into my DMs. Good, he's up.

> Hey, sugarplum. Why aren't you sleeping?

I can't wipe the sappy grin off my face at the cutesy nickname he uses for me when we're alone. He never says it in front of the other two, and I make a mental note to ask him why. I won't admit, even to myself, the feelings that these men stir inside of me.

> Hey, handsome. I could ask you the same question. The sun is barely up.

It's probably not a good idea to flirt too heavily with him this early in the morning. I might end up inviting him over to distract me so I can work out what to do about this invitation.

> Eh, you know me. I sleep a few hours at a time. I'm sure I'll catch a nap later. You're welcome to join me.

Yes, please. I'd been hoping to stay with them tonight, but I have a limited time to make this decision, and if I'm leaning toward yes, I have to be at the docks for the audition.

Am I leaning toward, yes? Maybe. After dreaming about being chased by faceless monsters for making the wrong decision, I'm still not sure. Perhaps some time alone with Will is just what I need. Since they already figured out my cam girl persona, there's no real reason to keep them out of my apartment anymore. It's not like he'll find my secret room unless I show him. I could just invite him over.

> *What if you come join me right now? We could snuggle.*

I know that he loves snuggling as much as I do. I change into a skimpy pajama set while we chat, because I'm certain he won't pass up the chance to finally get in my apartment.

> *You want me to come to your apartment? I didn't think anyone was allowed in there. Don't you have your enemies held captive or something?*

I laugh out loud at his joke. If he only knew how close he was to being right. Of course, I would never bring the men I target into my home. I'm much more comfortable taking them out in their own spaces.

> *Is that a no, then?*

I tease him, knowing that he won't turn me down, no matter how surprising my offer is. I'm tempted to send him a sexy pic of me, but I don't think I'll have to.

> *I'm on my way.*

I smile at the response.

Less than five minutes later, there's a quiet knock at my door. My apartment isn't messy, but I probably should have cleaned it a bit better. Too late now. Besides, I don't really have many material things. I check the peep hole before opening the door slowly. "Good morning. Can I help you, sir?"

Will scoops me up in his arms and forces his way into my home, closing the door quietly behind him. "I'm here to help you, ma'am. I heard you were low on cuddles and could use a refill."

I laugh and point toward my bedroom. "I can't believe you actually invited me over. This is a huge step for us, sugarplum."

"About that," I say, squinting at him.

"What?" he asks as he tucks us both into my bed and pulls me close.

"Why do you only call me sugarplum when we're alone or in texts?" It shouldn't matter, but I'm dying to know.

"I didn't know if it would make you uncomfortable for me to do it around the guys. I guess I was just keeping it our special thing," he says, running his fingers through my blonde hair. This man melts me.

I straddle him and capture his mouth with mine. I don't want to admit to any of them how attached I'm getting. It's not possible to have a real, serious relationship with three guys, is it? Especially if I'm a hired killer who can't tell them about my abilities.

"I don't know why you guys want me. I'm kind of a mess," I admit, not holding back my thoughts for once. I just don't go into details. I see the moment Will realizes that I'm not guarding myself the way I usually do. I want to pull back and hide from him, but it's too late.

He tucks a stray strand of hair behind my ear. "Sugarplum, you are not a mess. And we want you because you're awesome. I wish you could see that." Will kisses me again, all passion and desire. Somehow, I know he's not trying to get me naked though, even if that's what I want. This is bigger than just sex, and I'm terrified. I can handle sex; I'm not sure I can handle falling in love.

I was worried about choosing or rejecting the guild because of how it would affect my life. But how will that decision change things with the guys? I don't want to make the wrong choice and ruin what could be the perfect relationship.

At the same time, can I really turn down this opportunity? Fuck, I wish I had someone to talk to about this. I want to spill it all to Will, but I know I can't. Knowing everything would put him in danger, and I cannot do that. I don't need comfort that badly.

I've spent so long alone that I can't seem to let anyone in. Given my choice of profession, it makes sense. But it's not like I really chose this. Death and vengeance found me, not the other way around. And I have enough money now that I really could walk away from it all. I'd live comfortably for the rest of my life. I could settle down and have kids; raise a family; get a normal job. But is that the life for me? I wish I knew.

Will pulls me down beside him, tucking me under his arm, and resting my head on his chest. I feel safe here. I don't want to lose this. "You don't have to tell me what's bothering you. Just know that whatever it is, I'm not going anywhere. Neither are Jeremy or Luke. We're here for you; always."

He reaches down and wipes a tear from my cheek. What the fuck? I'm crying. I never cry. What is this man doing to me? The thought of losing him or the other two breaks my heart. Can I trust his words? I want to, more than anything.

"Take my mind off it. I can't talk about it right now. Are you sure that's okay?" The words flow out of me. I immediately want to take them back. This is the most vulnerable I've been around any of them, and I don't like it. Why do I need his approval so badly?

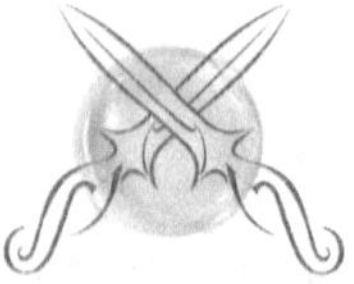

WILL

I know something is up with Em, and she admits that she doesn't want to talk about it. I should let it go. I have to let it go. I can't force her to tell me what's wrong if she doesn't want to. I wish that she could trust me, trust us, more than she does. As much as I want to push her to talk, I won't, because that's not what she wants right now. It doesn't seem to be what she needs, either.

It's hard seeing her vulnerable like this, but part of me likes it. Maybe this is what she needs; to have alone time with each of us so she can be more comfortable sharing herself. I'll have to talk to the guys about it and work out a schedule. I wonder if we should talk this over with her, but I don't want to scare her off. She's skittish about commitment, and I can tell that she's not comfortable discussing relationships.

I'll admit I was shocked when she texted and invited me over. I threw on clothes and raced down here before she could change her mind. She's never let any of us into her apartment before. I'm sure if I asked why, she'd claim it was because of her cam girl lifestyle, but that's a lie. She's hiding more than that. And whatever those secrets are, that's what keeps her from letting us in.

Right now, she wants a distraction, but she needs a shoulder. I'm not sure how to give her what she needs, so I'll give her what she wants. I turn toward her and cup her face, bringing her lips up to meet mine. "I'll take care of you." I don't mean to whisper the words, but once they're out, I can't take them back. I kiss her deeply, giving her everything I have.

I am falling for this girl so hard, but I can't tell her that, because it will scare her off. I know Jeremy and Luke feel the same way. We've talked about it, and the fact that she doesn't want to hurt us by choosing one over the others. The three of us are okay with sharing. We just have to convince her that this is what she wants.

EMILY

For a moment, I think Will is going to press me to talk about this. I have no idea what I would tell him. I can't admit that I'm an assassin. He'd never understand why I'm so comfortable taking men's lives for money. None of them would. They'll think I'm a monster. Hell, sometimes *I* think I'm a monster.

Then Will's lips are on mine, and my mind goes completely blank. This is just the distraction I need to clear my head and make this decision.

Part of me is dying to give myself over to my desire. I want to belong to these men. But I have to protect them from my dark side. I can't fully let them in, because what I do makes me a potential target for those who want to get away with their crimes. They deserve better. Can I be so selfish that I'll take the comfort he offers without giving anything more than pleasure in return? Yes, I can. And I will. I'll deal with the guilt later, after I've taken what I need and made my decision.

Kissing Will is different this time, and I feel like we've turned a corner. Things are changing between us, and I'm not ready. I have to pull back, but I need this time with him. I'll hate myself for using him later. For now, I'm going to enjoy everything about this.

I fist my fingers in his auburn hair while he kisses down my neck and collarbone. He pushes me back against the pillows and slides his hands down my body. I shiver at his touch anxious for our first one-on-one experience. I expect him to take my tank top and shorts off, but he doesn't. It's obvious he's planning to tease me before he finally gives me what I want.

Will pinches my nipple through the thin fabric and I arch my back. I want him to touch me without anything between us, but he's not finished taunting me yet. He settles his body on top of me, between my legs, and I can feel his erection as it presses against me. I roll my hips to feel more of him.

He groans and bites my shoulder. Tingles shoot through me, straight to my clit. I drag his shirt over his shoulders and drop it on the floor. His skin is warm against mine, and my body hums, confirming that this closeness is what I need. He kisses me as I rake my nails down his back.

I contort my body, pulling my feet up to grab the waistband of his shorts, then stretch my legs, taking his shorts and underwear with them. He breaks our kiss, laughing. It was an absurd move for sure, but it doesn't dampen our desire. "Sorry, you had my arms blocked. I had to get creative." I smirk at him before drawing him back down into another kiss.

He hums his approval and finally slides a hand under my shirt. I release a sigh at the touch of his skin on mine. "You're wearing too many clothes now," he growls against my neck. I gasp as he rips my tank down the middle, baring my chest.

"Will!" I exclaim. He covers my mouth with his hand for a moment and shakes his head.

"I'll buy you a new one. And shorts too," he says, shredding my shorts instead of trying to take them off me. I'm soaked from how hot this new side of him is getting me. Will is usually my sweet boy, but I could get used to him being forceful.

"I want to do something different, but you have to promise that you'll stop me if it weirds you out," he whispers in my ear as his fingers find my clit.

"Okay, I'm game for different. What is it?" As distracting as the sensations of pleasure are, I want to know what he's thinking of doing, and why he thinks it will freak me out.

He eases away from me a little and holds up his arm. It shifts from a human arm to a tentacle, complete with suction cups.

My eyes go wide, and my breath hitches. I don't know yet what he wants to do with that, but I am definitely into it.

"Yes, please," I respond to what I'm seeing. I should probably ask what he's planning, but I'm too distracted. Will smirks, then reaches for my breast with the tentacle. The small suction cups feel strange on my skin, but the way he tugs on my nipple sends sparks through me. He's never shifted during sex before, and I'm realizing that this might be my new favorite thing.

The tentacle slides down my body, suction cups sticking and pulling at my skin. Will raises me up a little so I can watch as it reaches my mound. A moan escapes me when the tentacle dips inside my center, then moves to my clit, dragging my wetness with it. I wonder for a moment if I should be weirded out by this, but it's Will's hand, just in a different form.

I trust him and I want this more than I would have expected. He alternates thrusting the tentacle into me and rubbing my clit until I'm squirming and on the verge of my release. "Mmm, Will, that feels so good."

He stops just before I come, dragging the tentacle up my body and teasing my nipples with it. I try to reach for his cock, but he grabs my hands and pulls them over my head. I play struggle against his grip, bucking my hips when I can't get free.

Will shifts his arm back to normal, then lines himself up and thrusts into me. His balls slap my ass, and he adjusts me so he can go even deeper. I meet him, thrust for thrust, our bodies slamming together in the punishing rhythm he sets. Every thrust pushes me closer to my release. He moves faster and pounds into me harder. I try to take control, but he doesn't let me. He keeps me pinned against the bed as he thrusts into me over and over.

I cry out when I come and feel the moment he joins me in ecstasy. I lay there for a moment with his weight on top of me. It's warm and comforting, reminding me of the pleasure we just shared. As much as I don't want to move, we should clean up so there's not a sticky mess in my bed later. I crawl out from under Will and pad to the bathroom. After cleaning myself up, I bring a warm cloth back with me for him to wipe off with.

"You're not kicking me out now, are you?" he asks with a sad smile. I hate that he expects me to ask him to leave after what we've just done.

I shake my head. "No. I thought we were taking a nap." He grins at my response, dressing quickly and settling back in my bed. I grab another set of pjs from my dresser, putting them on before joining him. Once we're snuggled up, I have no problem falling asleep.

WILL

I wait until Emily is almost asleep to whisper the words, I'm desperate to say. "I love you." I know if I tell her when she's fully awake and can respond, she'll run from me. We've all tried to get her to talk about her childhood, but she refuses. All we know is that it was tough, and she says that thinking about it gives her nightmares. I think that's why she's so adverse to feelings.

It's clear that she's never really had someone take care of her or love her. The guys and I want to change that, but it's a very slow process. I know that Jeremy and Luke both feel the same way I do. None of us have been brave enough to tell Emily, though. We don't want to chase her off.

Holding her in my arms, I let myself relive what we just did as I drift off to sleep. I'm awakened a few minutes later by Em thrashing and crying out in her sleep. I'd hoped that having me with her would ease the nightmares, but it doesn't look like I'm helping.

"It's okay, sugarplum. I've got you," I whisper. I press a kiss to her forehead. She whimpers and snuggles closer before calming down. I'm relieved, but don't think I'll get back to sleep now. I look around her room as the sun streams in through the partially closed blinds.

It's pretty bare in here. She has a bed and dresser, but not much else. Her nightstand and a chair in the corner complete the furnishings. I wonder if the rest of the apartment is the same. I was too caught up with her letting me in earlier to pay attention. That and the sexy little shorts set she answered the door in were way more important to focus on.

I wonder if she'll let me buy her some furniture or decorations; something to make this place more her own. Or if I can talk her into just moving in with us upstairs. That would make everyone happy. But there's a chance she'll run when I make the suggestion. Maybe I can find a way to make it her idea.

I know that the four of us need to have a talk. The guys and I want Emily to be ours, but she's been so distant. I hope that her cam girl identity is the only thing holding her back. I feel like there's more that she's hiding, but I don't want to push her away by digging too deep.

After snuggling closer and pulling Emily against me, I finally drift back to sleep. She sighs against my chest, and I'm certain I've chased away her nightmares for at least today.

JUST ANOTHER JOB

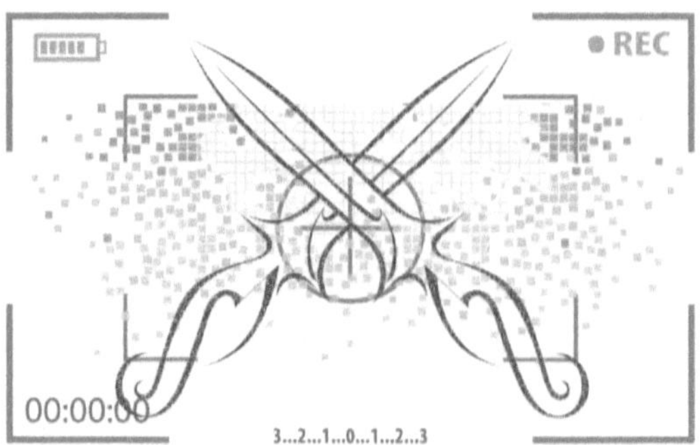

EMILY

I hear Will's whispered declaration as I'm drifting off to sleep. Panic wells in my chest, but I can't dwell on the issues that will cause, because I have a decision to make, and I desperately need to rest. I won't let myself react to his words, or the feelings they trigger. *I love you, too.* I can't say it; I can't even think it.

I let sleep take me, briefly considering that my nightmares may come back. At least I've warned the guys about them. So, if I have one, Will should understand.

My first dream seems normal enough. The faceless guild members chase after me, attempting to kill me. Just a day in my life, right? I run from them as fast as I can, wondering why I'm not shifting. I can't find anything electronic to slip into anyway, so it's pointless. I dodge attacks and just when I think I'm safe, the arrows start flying past my head.

I cry out as an arrow pierces my chest and hear Will's voice. "It's okay, sugarplum. I've got you." And fuck if that doesn't chase the nightmare away. My body relaxes and I sleep dreamlessly for a while. Then everything changes.

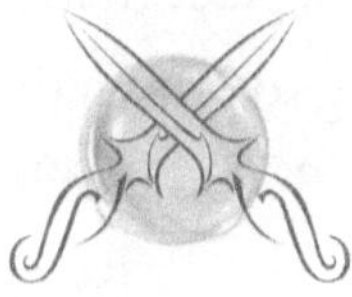

Suddenly I'm transported in time. Once again, I'm standing in the run-down warehouse my father took me to that day. How many times do I have to relive that day? My childhood wasn't an easy one. My mother was killed when I was small, and my father used me as slave labor until I hit puberty. That's where I am right now. Thirteen years old and standing in front of a man I've never met. Even though I remember what happened, it feels as if I'm there, going through it all over again. I'm that little girl I was and can't escape.

"You belong to me now, girl. Put this on," he growls, tossing a thin scrap of fabric at me.

"Where did my dad go?" I ask. Even though I lived it before, I'm not prepared for the hand to shoot out. The sting of his palm against my cheek brings tears to my eyes.

"Your dad sold you to me. You're mine now, and you will do what you're told. Put this on before I decide to really punish you," the man growls again. I pick up the cloth and stare at it. There is no way I'm doing what he demands. I've read about these transactions. I know he'll kill me if I don't cooperate, but I don't care. Death will be better than what this man has planned for me.

"No. If you want me to do as you ask, you'll let me talk to my dad first." I'm not in a place to make demands, and I know it. But I'm also not going to put on the thin strips of cloth this stranger just handed me. I won't do it; no matter what it costs me.

It doesn't take long to learn what he'll do about my refusal. First, he slaps me again. When I shake my head, he punches me. The moment his fist connects with my face, I know that he's lost control. I'm too small to stop him; I can't defend myself against this giant and his blows.

The man's fists pound into me, hitting my face, my chest, my legs. Blocking his hits doesn't help. He punches and kicks me until I'm curled into a ball in the floor. I'm broken. He might kill me after all. Pain lances through me, and I don't know if I can survive this. I have a plan, but might have pushed too far already. I close my eyes tightly and wait for him to stop beating me.

When more pain doesn't come, I look around the room and find that I'm alone. My only chance at survival right now is if I can shift. I didn't tell my dad when my powers revealed themselves, because I knew that he'd find a way to exploit me with them. Here I am, in a strange place, with powers that no one knows about. I might be able to survive this after all. It's my only chance.

I flex my fingers, wincing at the agony that accompanies the movement. My shift is difficult and takes longer than I want. After a few long, painful minutes, I'm pixelated and can move again. I'm still injured, but in this form I'm more able to push it away. Something about turning into pixels makes my soul feel better; stronger, even. The door stands open; my captor is obviously convinced that he's incapacitated or killed me. I follow the hallway to another room where I hear voices.

"You sold her to me! You told me she was trained! But she wouldn't get dressed like I told her to. So, I had to beat the shit out of her because she won't do what she's told. You lied, and I want my money back!" the man who beat me yells at my father.

The man who should have protected me stares at the much larger man standing in front of him. It's strange to me, but there's no fear. He doesn't hesitate, stabbing the knife I hadn't seen into my attacker's chest. "You son of a bitch. Now I have to waste money getting her healed so I can sell her again. I suppose you won't mind if I keep what you paid me, though, since you won't be needing it."

I should be shocked at the fact that my father just killed a man. Instead, I'm focused on the words he said as he did it. I freeze at my father's words. He's going to sell me again. No. I can't let that happen; I won't. I have to stop him from doing this to me or anyone else. I dart forward in my shifted form, determined to figure out a way to stop him.

He turns toward the door as I move and I slide right through him. My hands tighten into fists in front of me at the sensation, and the moment he's behind me, I feel something warm and wet in my hands. Looking down, I see his still beating heart resting on my pixelated palm. I just killed my father. A myriad of emotions overwhelms me, and I stare at the heart in my hand as it slowly stops beating.

"What the fuck?" he gasps, falling to the floor. A crimson puddle forms under him, and my father doesn't move. I look at the heart in my hand again before crushing it between my fingers. He'll never hurt anyone again.

Once I figure out how to get home, I take time to heal. Then I go through his belongings and discover that he'd been running a trafficking ring for years. He was responsible for kidnapping and selling young girls into the sex trade since before I was born. Not only was my mother one of his victims, but Mama's mysterious death was at his hand. I'm glad I was the one to finish him off.

Soon after, I discover that I can travel in my pixelated form along internet lines, which makes it easier to take out everyone who worked with my father. And since I have his list of suppliers and buyers, I work my way through it, learning how to kill as I go.

With this ring of evil destroyed, I discover that I have a talent for taking out sickos. Thus Umbr4g3_R0gu3 was born. I spend time learning how to control my powers, using my father's blood money to fund my endeavors. I should feel guilty, but I don't. I'm proud of myself for protecting those women and children.

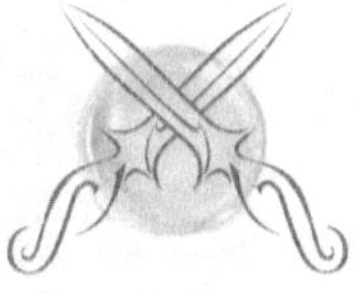

I wake from the strange dream with Will still wrapped around me. I'm surprised the nightmare didn't wake him. It's always violent and usually leaves me shaking. This time I'm calm, and I think it has to do with Will's presence.

It's both comforting and disturbing to have him here. I can't be upset with him; I asked him to stay. If I'm honest with myself, I want him here. I want all three of them here. But it's not fair to them for me to be that selfish. I should let them go so they don't get tangled up in my drama. My life is no place for love, or anything resembling it.

Looking at the alarm clock, I realize that I slept later than I'd expected. I have only twelve hours left to make my decision. With the knowledge that this guild is a life-long commitment, and they'll kill me if I get accepted and try to leave, I know I need to consider my options carefully. This isn't an offer I'll get again if I refuse. But am I ready to join a group like this? I'm not sure. What I do know is that this decision will be life changing. There's no turning back, no matter what I decide.

I reach out with my powers and check my phone while setting an alarm for eleven-thirty tonight. If I haven't made my final decision by then, I'll at least have time to get to the docks if I want to go through with it. I have texts from Luke and Jeremy. Neither knows where Will is, and they're concerned because he doesn't ever leave without a note or message.

> *Will is with me. We're fine. Nap time ran longer than expected.*

> *I'll send him home as soon as he wakes up.*

When I get their responses, I realize the mistake I've made.

> *Wait, Will is in your apartment right now?*

Jeremy asks.

> *I didn't think we were allowed in your apartment! What the hell?*

Luke is clearly upset, and I know I'm going to have to make it up to both of them later.

> *I couldn't sleep, and he was the only one up.*

> *We can have a slumber party here later. Okay?*

I don't want them to think I care about Will more than I do them. I hope they all understand that I need different things from time to time, and they'll each get time alone with me. I don't want to text all that, though, so I figure we can talk about it tonight at dinner.

> We're still on for dinner, right?

> Of course.

> Have you decided which option you'd like?

Shit. I forgot I was supposed to pick where we go tonight.

> Surprise me? You know I'd rather stay home than go out anyway.

I hope Jeremy doesn't get upset at my lack of desire to choose. I just don't have a preference between pizza, bar food, and the fancy restaurant. I'd be happy just hanging out at home with them. Did I just refer to their apartment as home? Fuck, I'm more screwed than I realized. I've let myself get more attached than I planned. Is this what I want? Why do they seem to get to me no matter how much I hold back?

With dinner mostly taken care of, I snuggle back in against Will. The warmth of his body eases my anxiety about the nightmares I had this morning while we slept. I can't think about what he said to me as I was falling asleep. I have bigger things to consider right now.

Should I accept the guild invite? Best case, I have a job for life. And I spend that life killing men who deserve it. Maybe women too, I don't really know. It's not like gender plays a part in someone being a monster. They clearly know about me, and claim that they won't send marks I would be against killing. But how can I trust a faceless organization that I don't know much about?

Worst case, I let this opportunity pass me by. It's not like I actually need the money. I've amassed a small fortune since my first kill at thirteen. In some ways it was easier when I was young. I could infiltrate the rings from the inside and take them all out. Now I have to play the part that I no longer completely fit into. I'm capable and stealthy, though, so it hasn't stopped me yet.

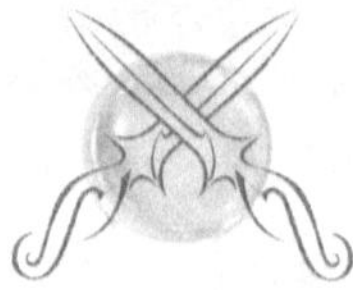

After Will wakes up, I try not to rush him to leave. I have another job to start and would prefer to do my cam work when he's not around. I know they've all seen my general subscription stream, but the one-on-ones are a little different. I don't need an audience for that.

"Are you sure you don't want to come upstairs with me?" he asks. It's hard to resist his sweet smile, but I have to work. Okay, I don't *have* to work, but I want to. My mission in life is bigger than our relationship.

"I've gotta get ready for work. And I can't have you down here distracting me. I'll see you guys for dinner." I kiss him, then give him a little shove toward the door. Reluctantly, he leaves. I lock the door and head to the bathroom to get dressed and put on my makeup.

When I have everything just the way I want, I pull my wig on and comb the hot pink curls into place. I stroll out of the bedroom in the lace babydoll with a matching satin robe over it. My aesthetic today is candy colored, because this mark prefers younger girls. I'm sure that's why I relived how I got here in my dreams this morning; I was anticipating this moment. I have to pretend to be what my father had hoped I'd become when he sold me for a profit.

I close my eyes, take a deep breath, and remind myself that I am in control here. I can back out of this job at any time. I decide where the video call goes, and I have the power to shut it down if things get uncomfortable. I am not the helpless underage girl I'm portraying. I cannot let myself forget that.

I settle myself on the bed and switch on my cameras. A few settings tweaks, and the screen shows everything around me a sweet candy pink, contrasting with the hot pink wig and nightie I'm wearing. Big_Dick_73 (what kind of username is that anyway?) should join the video call any minute. I don't know his real name, nor do I need to. My dark web contacts mysteriously referred him to me because of his eclectic tastes in cam videos.

My mark is on time, and research begins slowly. This time he's calling from his office, which is one of the places I need to access. I establish a link easily, and distract him as I play the part of an innocent girl who doesn't understand exactly what's on this creep's mind. He tells me how to touch myself as he watches, and I do it, feigning a purity I've never had.

When I've reached my breaking point, we schedule another call for next week. He's anxious to see me again, wanting more time today. Why do they always want more? I can't indulge him, though, insisting that I have other clients who are expecting me. When I promise to wear his favorite shade of blue next time, he finally agrees. I hold back a sigh, knowing that the next call will be the last time I see him. Well, it'll be the last time he sees me. I'll see him when I rip his tongue out for the filthy things he's said to me when he was pretending I was underage.

As soon as the call ends, I sneak into his computer and find the files I'm looking for. I quickly copy them onto a thumb drive and return to my apartment. With that finished, I can focus on my decision at hand, and figuring out what to wear for my dinner date.

> *I'm not asking where we're going tonight (I meant it when I said 'surprise me') But I do need to know what to wear…jeans, a dress, what?*

While I'm waiting for a response, I shower, cleaning all the body glitter and makeup off, then dressing in lounge clothes. I flop on my bed and pull out the invitation. The glowing white letters stare up at me as I remove the hot pink paper from the matching envelope once more.

It's mesmerizing to look at, and I wonder again how the guild managed to deliver this invitation. Someone was inside my apartment but didn't get caught by my security system. I dash from my bed to the small hidden room inside my cam space. Once inside, I pull up the video feeds from last night.

Sure enough, there was a brief period of time when my system was taken offline while I was delivering the proof of the Davis job being finished. But it wasn't long enough for someone to get from the door to my bedroom and back. This still doesn't make sense.

Interesting. This guild must be pretty powerful if they can infiltrate my apartment with all of its security and not get caught. Seventeen hidden cameras, and nothing. That reminds me; I should probably delete the footage of Will and me from earlier. He wasn't aware of the cameras, and I didn't think to ask him if it was okay to record. Probably because that would have led to a myriad of questions that I don't really want to answer.

I watch the video before I delete it. Of course, watching it brings up all the feelings from during, and I end up taking matters into my own hands. I rub my clit and finger myself until I come, then delete the footage. I make a mental note to ask the guys later how they feel about being recorded, though. I know it will lead to more questions and I'll have to explain that I have an intricate security system. I don't know how I'll convince them that it's a perfectly normal thing to have that many cameras hidden in this small of an apartment, but that's a later me problem. Maybe they'll be okay with it, since I am a helpless woman living on my own. I nearly fall out of my chair laughing at that thought.

With that problem solved, I lock the hidden room back up and stroll back to the bedroom. I have a few hours until our date, so I flop back on the bed and stare at the invitation again. I wish there was a clear answer here. Sometimes having free will is frustrating. It's my decision, and I have to make it. I don't have anyone to discuss the pros and cons with, so it's all on me.

I make a mental list, again. Pros: lifelong work, taking out people who deserve it, unlimited funds and equipment, recruiting my own team. Cons: FOMO if I refuse, no retirement, being hunted down if I fuck up. That's about as simple as I can make it. If only I knew who sent the invite, I'd have someone I could ask all the questions that are bouncing around in my brain. Can I really assume that I'll be selected? After all, it's just an audition. There's no guarantee they'll even want me after they see what I can do.

I shake my head, pushing that thought away. Of course, they'll want me. I can do things most other people can't. And recruiting my own team sounds promising. It's too bad the guys can't be part of that team. It wouldn't be fair to drag them into this, though, if that's what I decide.

None of that really matters. Being worried about my guys won't change things. Wait, *my guys?* Fuck, I'm in deeper than I thought. If I'm already thinking of them as mine, it may be too late to walk away. Can I break my own heart just to protect them? I don't know. As strong as the desire to protect them is, my desire to be near them is stronger.

I don't really know what love feels like. No one has been kind to me since my mother died—until I met Jeremy, Will, and Luke. It was instant attraction, and a seamless bond. We've been hanging out for months, but we talked about it and agreed that it needed to stay casual. Their fathers are important businessmen and wouldn't appreciate a scandal of their sons all being involved with the same woman. And I'm terrified of commitment.

I'll never admit that to anyone else, but there's no reason to hide it from myself. If I give myself over to this emotion, will I lose the parts that make me who I am? I know there's a chance that loving the three of them and letting them love me will make me stronger, but what if that's not what happens?

As much as I don't want to let them go, I don't want to put them at risk, either. My job is dangerous. That's a great excuse, but is it really that dangerous? No one, besides the guild, has ever figured out who I am and what I do. Why am I so worried about that now?

And if I'm really being honest with myself, wouldn't it be better to have the power of the guild behind me, if something did happen? Sure, I don't have a way to contact them, but if they really do see everything, they'll just know when I need backup.

I look at the clock. Almost eight hours left before I have to make this decision. I don't have to figure this out right now. But really, the decision is made, isn't it? There's only one logical choice. All that's left is to seal it.

I still have some time before our date, so I figure I'll make a quick trip to the docks and see if I can get this audition over with early. Hopefully it won't be anything too complicated.

When I arrive at the docks, I have no idea where exactly I'm supposed to go. I walk around the concrete lot, looking down the rows of shipping containers that are stacked in neat rows. This is ridiculous. If this is the audition, I'd probably be better off leaving now.

With that thought, I turn to leave and run directly into a slim, pink-haired figure with pale white skin. They seem to almost glow. The contrast of the hot pink waves that fall to their shoulders and the pale skin is interesting. I can't tell if this person is a man or woman.

"That's the idea, Emily. You don't need to know." They lock eyes with me, but their mouth doesn't move. I hear the words in my head.

"What? How?" I ask, unable to form complete thoughts.

A smirk crosses their face, and I'm mesmerized. They're beautiful in an ethereal way. I find myself moving closer until we're almost touching. "I'm Brynn. I was hoping you'd join us." They turn and walk away, and I'm certain that I'm meant to follow. So, I do.

We step inside one of shipping containers, and it's like I've been transported to another realm. Hell, I probably have. "Where are we?" I ask as Brynn stops walking in front of me.

"Your audition, love, where else?" they answer. I should be upset that they've answered my question with a question, but I'm entranced.

"What's my audition?" I mutter, turning to look around the room.

Brynn's eyes lock with mine, and they smirk again. A single word echoes in my brain. "Survive."

And just like that, I'm thrust into my nightmare. Half a dozen masked people come at me. A few have daggers, a couple brandish swords. I glance around the room, looking for something I can use to give myself an advantage.

I don't see anything right away that I can use. Instead of standing still and letting myself be targeted, I decide to find somewhere to hide while I make a plan of attack. I'll have to defeat them one-on-one if I want to get out of here. And I need to do it quickly, because I have a date tonight.

Part of me is pissed that Brynn didn't give me any warning about this, and part of me likes the challenge. I don't normally take out six people at once, or even in the same night. I decide to use my attackers' lack of knowledge against them. They don't know me, and won't be expecting what I can do.

One of them stumbles upon my hiding spot, thrusting a dagger at me. I don't hesitate, shifting my arm and thrusting my hand into the man's chest. I have no reason to kill him, so instead of ripping his heart out, I collapse his lungs. It's painful, I'm certain, but will incapacitate him without being fatal.

With the success of that move, I decide that's how I'll take them all out. I shift the rest of my body into pixels and slowly move across the room, hunting my prey. It's slower than I want, but without electronics or internet lines, I don't have much choice. I feel safer in my shifted form, and have less chance of being caught.

Once I've dispatched three more of my would-be attackers, I move toward where Brynn is watching the action. Hovering behind them, I whisper, "Is there a reason you want me to kill these people? Or do you just like playing God?"

They spin around, shocked that I'm able to get so close without them noticing written on their face. "Oh, you are a slick one," Brynn says, actually speaking the words aloud this time. "I think you'll fit in quite nicely. I'm also pleased that you didn't just kill my soldiers without cause. I can't tell you how many I've had to replace over the years with these auditions."

"Does that mean this is over? Or do I need to take out the other two?" I feel like all I'm doing here is asking questions, and it's starting to annoy me.

My host nods, then turns back toward the room and claps their hands once. "Okay, people, I have what I need. We're finished here. Please clean up before you leave." With that settled, they turn back to me. "I would like to extend an invitation to join us, if you are so inclined."

I return to my human form quickly. Even though I was certain this is how the audition would end, I'm still surprised by it. At this point, I can't say no. I knew that when I came to the docks. "I'm in." Suddenly a name pops into my head. "Who is Donovan?"

"Your first target, love. We don't need you to collect evidence; we've taken care of that already. Just do what you do." Brynn's voice sounds in my head again.

I nod, turning to leave. The moment I step out of the shipping container, a chill works its way up my spine. I just joined an assassin's guild, and I have my first target. I realize that I didn't get answers to most of my questions, but there will be time for that later.

I don't want to dwell on the guild right now. I need to return to my apartment and get ready for my date with the guys. Instead of walking back, I jog, arriving quickly and barely breaking a sweat.

Once I'm home, I have a little time to research before I need to leave. I return to my hidden room and investigate Donovan. He's a well-respected vampire who owns Donovan Industries. It's obvious to me that his business is a front for his illegal activities. I don't bother to check out articles that mention his family; they aren't part of this. Most of the time, it's easier to kill someone if you don't know about their loving wife and kids. Seeing a monster as anything else makes my job more difficult. Instead of focusing on the man, I dig into his kinks. Apparently subservient women are what get him off. As usual, I can pretend. I'm turning out to be a pretty good actress when I need to be.

I need to figure out how to get him on my books. As soon as the thought pops into my head, a new appointment request dings in my dark web calendar. Could it be that easy? I open my calendar and see that Donovan himself has requested a cam call. I guess it can be that easy. Looks like I'll be meeting him tonight. With any luck, I'll get everything I need and be able to end this quickly. Considering all I really need is a connection and a few minutes, I'm feeling pretty confident about this one. I've already verified his involvement in illegal activities—the same type as the men I regularly go after. So Donovan will fit right in with my other victims.

This job will be a little different from my others, because there was no request for documents or information. Donovan has to die, and I am the one chosen to handle it. Pride fills me, and I wonder for a moment if I'm actually a little sick and twisted. I love being the one who doles out the punishment to the men who are so similar to my father. It's thrilling to end their lives after I confirm that they are guilty of the illegal endeavors that created my fortune. Since I don't need to collect evidence, I may be able to kill this fucker tonight. I wonder if Brynn will be impressed with how quickly I plan to handle this target.

Yeah, I'm more than a little sick and twisted. But the world is a better place for what I do, and who says a person should do work they don't enjoy?

I realize that I'm running late now, but I can't be upset about it. I have a new mission, and I'm excited to see what's next with the guild. I check my texts to see if I got a response about what to wear while I shower, put on makeup, and fix my hair.

Jeans are fine. We're going casual tonight.

That tells me that Jeremy won the decision, and we're having pizza. Good. I prefer that to the fancy place Luke would have taken us anyway.

CHANGES

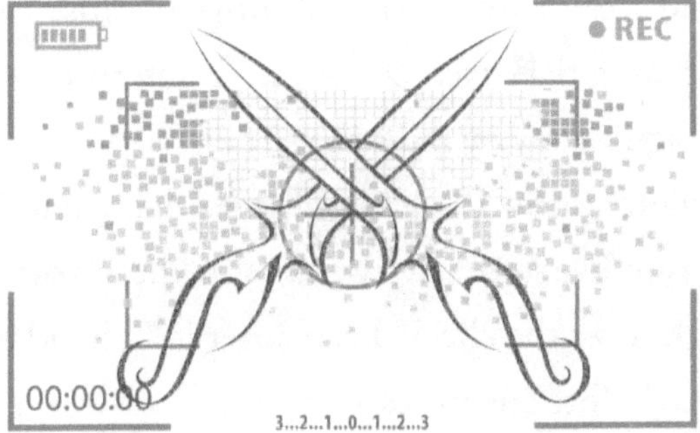

EMILY

Dinner ends up being exactly what I need to reset after everything that's happened the past few days. I'm not usually a fan of bowling, but this place does have amazing pizza. The guys get really cute when they compete, too, so that helps. I find myself playing down my abilities, though, and that bothers me. But after a couple of hours, I feel recharged and happy about spending time with my guys.

Until the check comes, and the guys argue about who's gonna pay. That's when I hear something that makes me rethink everything. Please tell me Jeremy did not just say what I think he did.

"Wait, what did you just say?" I ask, hoping I heard wrong.

"I said, 'Luke Donovan, you son-of-a-bitch, you can't keep showing off by paying for everything.' Why?" Jeremy responds.

No. No, no, no. Fuck. My next mark could be related to Luke. I can't let my shock register, or they'll figure out my secret. And I can't refuse the job now, because the guild is different than a dark web contract. Trying to back out now would be signing my own death warrant.

"I just didn't know Luke's last name," I laugh it off as if it's not the reason I've started to sweat. "You know, you guys don't have to fight over the check. I can cover it." I hand my card to the waitress before anyone can stop me.

My heart races and sweat drips down my spine. What am I going to do? That's a stupid question. I have no choice here. I'm going to kill Donovan, that's what I'm going to do. Then I'll worry about whether or not he's related to one of the guys I'm falling for, because if I know before, I may not be able to go through with it. And that could get ugly for everyone. It doesn't matter who he's related to anyway; Donovan has to die. If not, I'll be the one killed. And I'm not ready for that.

With the check issue finally settled, we head back to their apartment. "Will you come up with us for a bit, Em?" Luke asks.

Why does his question make me nervous? Did he somehow figure out that I'm an assassin for hire? How am I gonna explain all of this? I can't worry about these questions right now. Worst case, I'll excuse myself to the bathroom and shift to get away. But then I'll have to relocate and start over. I really don't want that. Especially since that would mean giving up these three amazing guys.

"Sure," I respond with a smile. "Is everything okay?"

Will wraps an arm around me as we head to the elevator. "Nothing to stress over. We just wanna talk to you about something."

His words make my heart jump. I don't want anyone else to profess their love for me, even if Will doesn't realize I heard him. It's not like I can stop them from saying whatever they want, though, so I'll just have to deal with it. This night just keeps getting more and more challenging.

I jump when the door closes behind us, and Jeremy laughs. "Someone is a little nervous to be alone with us tonight."

"I'm not nervous. The noise just startled me, that's all." I know they don't believe me, and I really hope that they don't keep pushing.

Luke drags me down next to him on the couch, then Jeremy settles on my other side. Will sits on the coffee table in front of me, and I feel like they've boxed me in. "What is this all about? I feel like this is an intervention, and I'm about to hear how you all care about me, but I have to stop doing what I've been doing." I try to make a joke, but their faces are serious. I swallow hard and wait for what comes next.

"You've been hesitant with us, and we know it's because of your secret," Jeremy begins.

My jaw drops. They know. Fuck. After so long of not being caught, how were they the ones who figured it out? I've been so careful. I never should have let Will into my apartment. That has to be how they figured it out.

"But now that we know about your cam work, you don't have to push us away anymore," Will continues.

I barely hold back a sigh of relief at Will's words. They don't know. Not about that.

"We just want you to give this relationship a chance," Luke insists. "The three of us are all in, and we want you to be as well."

"I don't know what to say. This is not what I expected," I admit. I figured there would be sweet words of love and desire, not practical reasoning when they finally brought this up. I can't argue with them now. Ugh.

"Then say yes. To at least giving this a chance. We'll be exclusive; just the four of us together in whatever way works for all of us. No competition, no jealousy. Please say you'll try it." Will looks as if he'll cry if I refuse. And if I'm honest with myself, I don't want to say no. I want to make this work with them. I'm just not sure it will. Can I give them all what they need? I have no idea. But I guess we're about to find out.

I take a deep breath, knowing that my answer won't be what they expect. "Okay." That one word changes each expression that stares at me. They go from concerned to confused, then settle on elated. It's clear they expected to have to convince me. I'm making this too easy for them. My heart does a little cartwheel, and I can't wipe the smile off my face, so I guess I've made the right decision. Now if I can only keep my secret life secret.

Luke kisses me, hard and sloppy. When he backs away, Will is there, kissing me tenderly with promises of the future. The moment our kiss breaks, Jeremy leans over and kisses me with so much passion that it takes my breath away. I shouldn't want this. I should run. I have to protect them from anything that could hurt them or break their hearts. And that includes me. I'm not good for these men, but I want them too badly to leave.

I hate feeling so conflicted. But these are my men now, and I will fight for them. Even if I end up being the one who destroys everything. I am a monster, after all.

Before I can get hung up on the commitment I just made, they each kiss me again, pulling my focus back to the moment. We end up in Luke's room tonight. He's fully embraced the vampire stereotype, with a coffin on display in the corner, and dark velvet curtains on the windows. None of it is necessary, because he has an enchanted ring that protects him from sunlight, and vampires don't actually sleep in coffins. That was an old wives' tale that got blown out of proportion, like the garlic and mirror things, and vampires only eating blood. Talk about stories designed to scare people. Of course, vampires feed on blood. But it's not nearly as much as the movies and stories make it look like, and it lasts them for a while.

As a matter of fact, Luke is obsessed with mirrors. He has one on every wall in his room, and a large one on the ceiling over the bed. The first time I came in here, I thought that he must be extremely vain. He's not. He just likes to watch everyone, and the mirrors are the best way to do it. Most of the time, when we're in here, Luke makes sure he's not the center of attention. Of course, usually, all three of them are focused on me no matter whose bedroom we're in.

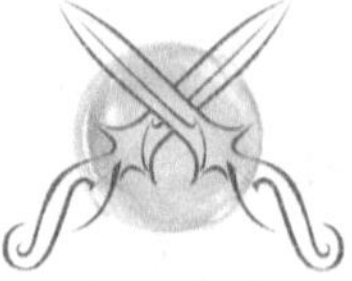

LUKE

Em is distracted, which is pretty normal for her. I wish I knew what she was thinking about as she surveys my bedroom. They all tease me about my vampire goth decorating, but it makes me laugh to embrace the silly stereotypes that humans put on us.

Since I know she won't tell us what's bothering her, I make it my mission to bring her focus back to the here and now. I won't make her feel self-conscious by calling her out on it, either. I nod to the guys and the three of us back her up against the bed. Jeremy drags her onto it while Will and I take her clothes off.

I plan to tease and taunt her until she's begging me to fuck her pretty pussy. I lick my lips as I stalk toward her. "You have your safe word?" I ask, my eyes devouring her.

She nods, and I shake my head. "Come now, kitten, you know I have to hear it."

"Dracula," she whispers with a chuckle.

"Good girl. Now, if things go too far, you just say that silly vampire's name, and I'll stop. Got it?" We don't play often, but

I need to know she won't let me hurt her. I enjoy biting and drinking her blood during sex. I don't enjoy harming those I care about.

Em nods her agreement, and I spread her legs apart to look at her. "Mmm, so beautiful." I click my fangs in place and watch her eyes go wide. She's not struggling or trying to get away. My kitten loves it when I bite her. I lean down and lap my tongue against her slit.

The moan that escapes her is delicious, almost as much as she is. I lick her again, then bite her thigh and suck—just a taste for now. I'm careful to lick the puncture wounds so they heal faster. Em cries out as she reaches her first orgasm. I can't wait to make her do that again and again. Her pleasure is my favorite drug, and I'm definitely an addict.

My cock strains against my jeans, begging to be set free. I can't do that yet, though, because I know the moment I do, I won't be able to hold back from sinking into her. I want to draw this out as long as I can. I run my tongue over her sex again, enjoying the way she arches her back. She's practically begging me for more already.

Will and Jeremy busy themselves with kissing our girl and teasing her nipples while I continue to worship her gorgeous pussy. I lick and suck at her, sliding two fingers inside to work her g-spot until she comes again. I want to make her beg for it, but I'm not going to be able to hold out long enough to make it happen. It's unfortunate, but we have the rest of our lives to play games.

Right now, I'm going to bury myself inside of her and fuck her senseless. I lean back enough to get out of my clothes. Em locks eyes with me, mesmerized by watching me strip. I give her a little show, then crawl back to my favorite spot between her legs.

I lift her up so Will can spread lube on her rosebud. Once he gets her ready, he lays back on the bed and I carefully ease Em down on his cock. She spreads her legs further apart to give us both access, and Jeremy groans as she grips his dick. The whole scene is hot to watch; even more being part of it.

With everyone else in place, I ease my cock into her, giving her a minute to adjust to being so full. When she nods that she's ready, Will and I thrust into her together. She cries out at the pace we set, but doesn't use the word that will stop everything. Her pleasure is the only thing that matters to me at this moment.

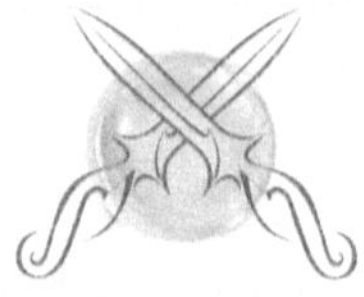

EMILY

Luke and Will thrust into me together a few times, and I have to brace my hands on the headboard to keep from banging against it. Jeremy slides his dick against my face, and I suck him into my mouth. The three of them work together to guide me toward my next orgasm. The feeling of their hard dicks thrusting into me over and over gets me there quicker than I'd like to admit, but they don't seem to mind.

I feel myself clamp down on Luke, determined to make him come with me. When he gets close, Luke leans down and kisses my neck. I know he'll wait to bite me until Jeremy is out of my mouth, because he worries that I'll need to use my safe word. I don't think he'll hurt me, though, so I'm not worried about it.

I don't know how much longer I can hold out, though, so I swirl my tongue along Jeremy's cock and suck harder. He thrusts into my mouth a couple more times, then I feel his release in the back of my throat. I swallow fast to keep up with it, licking him clean as he pulls away.

Just then, I come again, clamping down even harder on Luke and Will. They both come at the same time, and Luke's fangs pierce my neck. He takes a couple of long pulls of my blood, then forces himself to let me go.

The moment Will and Luke pull themselves from me, Jeremy is there with a warm rag to clean me up. He hands another to each of the guys. I'm always amazed at how caring they are with each other. Once we're all cleaned up, we snuggle in Luke's bed for a while. I know that they want me to stay, and as much as I want to, I can't. I have a job to do. The first part of that is to deal with Big_Dick_73. The second is to get ready for my cam call with Donovan.

I don't normally do two kills in a night, but I'm making an exception tonight, if I can. I still have a couple of hours before my call, and I can take care of the other guy after. I let myself relax with my guys for a little while. As soon as the three of them fall asleep, I sneak out of Luke's room, grabbing my jeans and shirt. I can find my panties and bra later. I throw on my clothes and head down to my apartment.

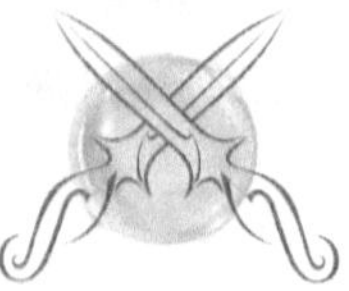

After a quick shower, I decide on my purple babydoll with my lavender wig for the meeting with Donovan. I know it's not his favorite color, but it is one Luke likes. I have to remind myself that no matter what this man's relationship with my lover is, he has to die. The contract has been accepted and cannot be turned down at this point. It's his life or mine, and I'm not giving mine up for a scum bag like this guy. Not when I've just found everything I ever wanted with my men.

I get everything set up with my security system and the cams to record our meeting. I carefully apply my makeup and put my mask on. With my wig in place, I settle on the bed and turn everything on. Donovan should be here in just a moment.

I don't have time for my heart to start racing and my breath to catch in my chest. I have to do the job. I can't worry about how this will affect anyone else, or if what I'm doing is right. This guy is a player in the trafficking ring I've been chasing, and I'll confirm that before I kill him. Either way, I will find out exactly why someone wants him dead before I do the deed.

The moment Donovan's face fills the screen, my eyes go wide. I force my expression to fit the mood of the call. I can't let him know that I recognize him. I don't have confirmation, but this man is definitely related to Luke. My sweet Luke, who just fucked me and drank my blood upstairs only an hour ago.

A few minutes of chit chat, and Donovan is asking to book regular weekly appointments. He explains his fetishes and asks for a demonstration that will prove I can accommodate his desires. Have you ever had to masturbate for a man you suspect is your lover's father? No? Just me then. Great. As awkward as the situation is, I don't think Donovan has realized that there's a problem.

I check the time and realize that we've actually gone over time. I have to establish my link to his system before he realizes and disconnects. I keep the show going another minute or two while I do what I need to. Once I have the entry point, I smile at him.

"Our time is up. But we can definitely make another appointment. Please be sure you pay immediately, so that you can get scheduled." I never let a regular schedule until they've paid for their last call, so it helps ground me in character to explain that to him. It doesn't matter that he'll be dead in a couple of hours.

"Absolutely, Jasmin. I'll pay now." He taps some buttons on his phone, and I receive an alert that the deposit went through.

"Thank you. It's been a pleasure. We'll talk soon." I shut the cam off before he can object, holding onto my connection with his computer. If I don't do this now, I won't be able to. He looks too much like Luke. If I spend any time thinking about it, I'll back out. And if I back out,

I barely make it into the secret room before I'm fully shifted into my pixelated form. I spend two minutes verifying that Donovan is indeed connected to the trafficking ring I've been chasing, then take a deep breath and float into the computer. I grab the files I need, tucking them away so I can have the proof I need if this ever comes up with Luke. I can't tell him that I'm the one who did this. Can I even do this? I'm not so certain anymore. But I have to. Otherwise, the guild will come after the guys, then kill me. Brynn didn't exactly say that, but it's what I expect if I ever cross them. I shake the thought away.

Donovan must die, and I will be the one to take him out. I've never let emotions complicate a job before. I'm not about to start now.

Sliding out of the back of Donovan's computer is easy. His set up allows me plenty of space to maneuver. It appears that his computer is in a room by itself. That's not a creepy perv move at all, buddy. I know from my research that Donovan is a vampire—even more evidence that he's Luke's dad—and there are actually several nice pieces of furniture I can destroy to stake him with.

Does he deserve an easy death? Not even a little bit. But when I see pictures hanging on the wall of what has to be a young Luke, I decide it's the best way to do it. Normally, I would plant the damning evidence where his family would find it. Then I would kill the asshole in the most painful way possible. Not this time.

This time, I'm showing mercy. He'll still die, just not in a way that will hurt his son any more than is absolutely necessary. I could search the house for him, then hunt him down, but I'm actually in a bit of a rush. I ping his cellphone and follow the response.

I find him in the shower, stroking himself and watching a recording of our call. Eww. I really have to make sure they can't record things from now on. I float back into the bedroom and slam an antique wooden chair on the floor to break it. I pick up a piece of the leg that will make the perfect stake, then head back into the bathroom.

Of course, the commotion of me breaking the chair interrupted his shower. Donovan has shut the water off and is stepping out, wrapping a towel around himself. Well, at least he'll be covered when he dies. I shift the stake in my hand and move closer.

"What the hell?" he asks as he walks into the bedroom and sees the broken chair. "Who the fuck did this? Do you have any idea how expensive that chair was?"

I stab the chair leg through his back and into his heart. It's a cowardly move, but I can't look him in the eyes and kill him. He looks too much like his son. The moment the stake pierces his heart, smoke starts to rise from his chest. I wonder if he'll combust, or if that's just a lie they tell to sell more books.

I watch as Donovan falls over, face down on the carpet. The smoke continues, but he doesn't go up in flames. So that was another rumor created by the media. That's good to know. I've finally killed my first vampire, but I don't feel great about it. I'm happy to have taken a monster off the streets. I'm just worried what this will do to my sweet vampire. I hate feeling so conflicted.

I don't know much about any of my guys' families, except that they all have money. The fact that it's tainted with the blood of those who didn't have a choice in their lives makes me sad for Luke's family. Nothing I found implicates any of them in his shady business dealings.

I double check that Donovan is indeed dead, then head back to my apartment. I still have another guy to take care of, and if I wait, I might break down and fail. As soon as I materialize in my safe room, I take a deep breath and shift back into my pixelated form. I have to finish this job. I can't let myself stop now.

I tap into Big_Dick_73's computer system and shoot toward him. I'm pushing my emotions away the best I can, but I know a breakdown is coming. Guilt eats at me for killing Luke's father. I try to justify it by reminding myself that he was a scumbag, but it's not working.

I slide out of the computer and come face-to-face with the man I'm looking for. He looks familiar, but I can't quite place him. After viewing the files on his computer again, it doesn't matter to me who he is. He's even higher up on the chain than Donovan was, so he has to die.

I grab him by the throat and shove him at the chair. He falls backward, sputtering. "What's going on? Who's there?" he stammers, his eyes searching the room for what he ran into. I glance sideways and see an envelope with a name on it.

"Mr. Matthews, I presume?" My pixelated form distorts my voice and I watch his eyes go wide in panic.

"It wasn't me. I didn't touch them. All I did was arrange transportation from one place to another. I never touched those girls," he insists.

You have to love a guilty conscience. He knew what he did was wrong but did it anyway and took money for it. Dumb fucker. Admitting it just pisses me off almost more than lying about it would. Like being honest will save his life or something.

"Ah, ah, ah, Matthews. You can't expect me to believe that you had nothing to do with it besides arranging transportation. You selected those girls. You photographed them. You sold them. And now you have to pay," I say, floating closer.

His panic grows, because he can't see me, and I'm not talking anymore. I shove my pixelated hand through his chest and grip his heart. He's going to die the same way my worthless father did, for the same reasons.

I crush his heart in my hand, then pull it out and drop it on the floor before sliding back into the computer and returning home.

BAD NEWS

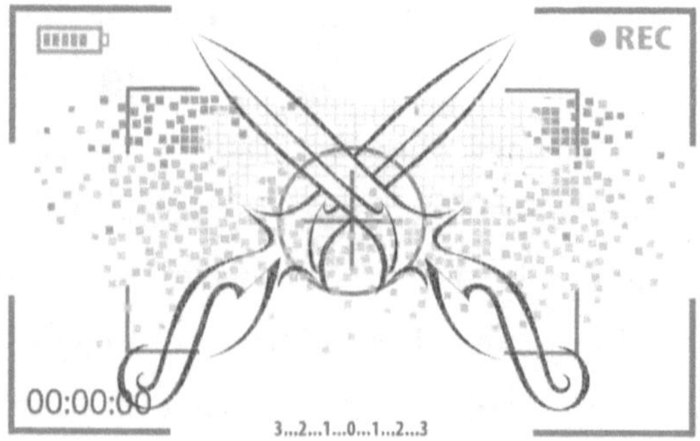

EMILY

I stay locked in my apartment and sleep off and on for two days. Guilt eats at me constantly, whether I'm awake or asleep. Nightmares haunt me—images of staking Donovan only to find out it was really Luke, or killing Donovan and turning to find Luke watching. The horror on his face is burned in my brain, even if it's only from my imagination.

I know I've gotten texts from Jeremy and Will, but I can't respond. Not yet. I have to pull myself together. Both Jeremy and Will explained that Luke's father was found dead at their family home, and that it looks like murder. *If only you knew,* I think, wallowing in my misery. It takes Luke's text to finally snap me out of it.

> I need you.

Those three words both bolster me and tear me apart. Would he still need me so much if I hadn't killed his father? I can't answer that. There's no way to know. But I don't think he would.

> I'll be there in ten.

I jump out of bed and shower quickly, thankful that I keep my blonde hair short. I don't bother with makeup or drying my hair.

I hate that I'm going to lie to them all, but I know I am. And they'll believe me, because I've given them no reason not to. I throw on a sweatshirt and leggings and race upstairs. I don't bother to knock because I know they're all home.

I rush inside, and three sets of eyes land on me. What I don't expect is for all three to be bloodshot and red-rimmed. They've all been crying. Shit. This is worse than I thought. What I've done is unforgivable. There is no way we'll be able to get past this if the truth ever comes out.

"I'm sorry. I was sick and didn't want to give it to you guys. I got all your messages when I started to feel better this morning." The lie rolls easily off my tongue. I've had a full forty-eight hours to come up with it, after all.

Luke holds his arms open and I fall into them on the couch. He pulls me into his lap and hugs me as if he's scared I'm going to get away. I hold him just as tightly, because I actually am scared he'll get away. If they ever find out—no, I can't think about it.

"I'm just glad you're here now. The funeral is this afternoon. Will you go with us?"

As much as I want to avoid the funeral of the man I killed, I can't say no to Luke's simple request. I nod, pulling his head to rest on my shoulder.

"Of course. Whatever you need," I offer.

"What we need is to find out who did this. Then we need to tear them apart for it," Jeremy growls. I've seen his wolf before but never when it's been rage induced. It's thrilling and terrifying. I don't think I could defeat him in a fight. I'm not even sure that shifting would allow me to escape him.

"Revenge is not the answer. Leave the police work to the cops, Jer. Everything happens for a reason, and we may never know what the reason for this is." Will sounds like the sage older brother, giving advice to his hot-head little brother right now.

"What do you think, Luke? Don't you want us to go after whoever did this?" Jeremy tries again to rile us up.

Luke shakes his head. "It won't bring him back. There's no point. If they find the guy who did it, sure, I'd love to see him get punished. But I won't be chasing him down myself."

My heart is breaking for him. I'm relieved that he doesn't want to hunt me down and tear me apart for what I've done. I can't help but wonder if it would make a difference; knowing it was me.

I don't have time to worry about it, because we have to get ready to leave for the service. Of course, it's at Luke's parents' house. I'm not worried about pretending I've never been there. I doubt they'll be giving tours. I'm also pretty confident that I'll be in a part of the house I've never seen.

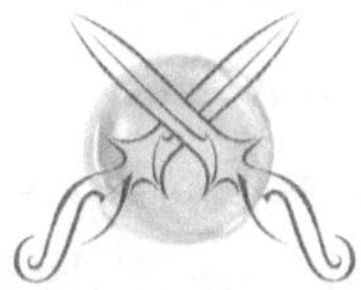

The service is quiet and reserved. Everyone here clearly has money and isn't afraid to use it for their whims. Luke keeps me by his side the entire time, with his fingers threaded through mine. It seems as if he expects me to run at any moment. Or maybe he wants an excuse not to shake hands with all of these people. I'm not sure. His hand grips mine tightly as people file in, giving their condolences. He nods respectfully, but barely speaks. I find myself thanking them all for him, and it feels weird.

Luke doesn't bother to introduce me to anyone, so unless they ask, I don't either. Jeremy walks over with a tall man who looks a lot like him. "Come on, Dad. I just want you to meet her. Then maybe you'll understand."

His dad barely looks up from the cell phone in his hand as Jeremy introduces us and I offer my hand. Mr. Franklin glances at it and says, "Yes, yes, very nice. I have to go."

I can't stop myself from tapping into his cell phone to see exactly what's so urgent that he can't give his son a moment of his time. The message surprises me, and I have to cough to cover my gasp. Someone has texted Franklin about Big_Dick_73's death. The only reason to do that would be if Franklin was also connected to the trafficking ring.

After he walks away, I turn to Jeremy and Luke. "Do you guys know a lot about your dads' businesses?" I try to sound casual, but I have to know if my guys are involved. I won't be able to protect them if they are. To be honest, I wouldn't want to. And I don't want to be involved if they end up on a hit list.

"My dad was a banker," Luke says. "He just helped people invest their money. Nothing too exciting."

Jeremy looks at me and grins. "My dad is the CEO of Franklin and Jeffries, the most prominent law firm in the city."

"Oh, that's exciting. Do either of them dabble in any other kind of business?" It's not like I can ask, 'Do you know what kind of kinky shit your dads are into?' because that's not exactly casual conversation. I can imagine their faces if I did ask that. It would not be pretty.

"They go golfing together all the time, with Will's dad, too. He's the other half of the law firm. Or they did go golfing together," Luke says. I don't want to push anymore because I can tell he's barely holding it together. Tears fill his eyes, and he turns away.

"I'm sorry, honey. I didn't mean to bring up more sadness. We can go home whenever you're ready. Unless you need to stay for your mom," I say, squeezing his hand. This is by far the most awkward situation I've ever been in, and I'm not sure that I'm helping Luke any.

"Yeah, I think I'd like to go home now. Mom has all these people here; she'll be fine," he responds.

After saying goodbye to his mom, Luke and I wait in the car for Jeremy to find Will. Apparently, his father needed to talk to him about a few things while everyone else was paying their respects. It didn't sound good, and I've been a little worried about him.

Once we're back at the guys' apartment, Luke decides to lay down for a while. I go with him to his room and help him into comfy pajamas. I tuck him into bed, and he pulls me on top of him.

"Will you stay with me until I'm asleep?" he asks. I nod, wrapping my arms around him and scooting to lay beside him instead of staying on top of him. "And will you still be here when I wake up?"

"I'll stick around, I promise. If I'm not in here with you, I'll still be in the apartment." The promise is easy to make. I have no plans to go anywhere else today. I need to be here as much as he needs me.

"Okay. Thanks for today. I don't think I could have made it through this without you." His words are meant to convey appreciation, but instead, I feel more guilt. This entire situation is my fault. If it wasn't for me, Luke wouldn't be laying here in his bed with a forlorn expression. Or would he? If I hadn't taken the position with the guild, who's to say that they wouldn't have sent someone else to kill Donovan? I have no way to know that for sure, but it still doesn't ease my guilt.

"It was nothing, really. I wish I could do more for you," I answer. I hold him as he finally lets his tears fall. My heart breaks for him. Luke rests his head on my shoulder and I rub his back while he purges his emotions.

I know he hasn't eaten today, and that he won't do so willingly. But he needs to keep up his strength. "Luke, you need to eat something. At least drink a little blood. Please." I hold my arm in front of his face and he shakes his head. "You can't let yourself suffer. Please, do it for me."

His eyes meet mine, and he gives me a sad smile. They stay locked on mine as he sinks his fangs into my arm and drinks deeply for a moment. I wish he'd take more, but he only drinks a little. Then he licks the punctures to help them heal and rests his head on me again.

"Thank you for taking care of me. I need you to know how much it means to me that you're here," he says. His words are quiet, and I can tell that he's starting to doze off.

"Shh, hush now and rest. I'll see you in just a bit." I brush his hair off his face, gently petting him until his eyes close and his breathing regulates. I know he's not asleep yet, because he keeps tapping on my leg. After a bit, I recognize the rhythm from a song he's fond of. I hope it helps him to relax a little. I kiss his forehead and continue to smooth his hair back.

When he finally falls asleep, I wait a few more minutes before untangling myself and heading to the living room. I want to check on Will. He didn't seem too excited about having to hang out with his dad during the services. I wanted to ask him about it earlier, but Luke needed me more.

I find him in the kitchen, making lunch. "Are you okay? Things seemed strained with your dad." I don't want to push, but I will if I have to. It's ridiculous that I expect them to be honest with me when I can't tell them the truth about anything.

"I'm fine. Sorry he wasn't very social. He's got a lot on his mind with what just happened to Luke's dad. As for our talk, he just expects a lot from me, and I'm not living up to my potential. It's frustrating for sure, but I can handle it. Dad's mad that I won't join the company. I'd rather not be stuck in a stuffy board room all day." Will seems annoyed with his dad, but not upset about the conversation.

"Oh, was that all? I guess that's not too bad," I admit, relieved that it wasn't more serious. "I thought maybe you were in trouble for something."

"He also told me that I could do better than sharing a trollop with my friends. But don't worry, I punched him for that one." Will's tone is so nonchalant that I almost miss what he says.

"Wait, what? Your dads know that we're all in a relationship together?" My eyes go wide, my chest constricts, and I feel like I'm going to throw up. This wasn't something I expected to be public knowledge.

"Of course they do. We're all proud of you. We don't have anything to be ashamed of, so we told our families about you. Is that a problem?" he asks.

"That does explain a few whispers and stares today." I pause for a moment, considering. "It's fine. If you guys aren't worried about it, I'm not either." I try to mean that. I don't care what other people think of me, but I don't want anyone talking shit about my guys. "Did you really punch your dad?"

"Of course I did. No one talks shit about our girl. He'll either respect you or I'll keep punching him. I told him as much, too."

"That's insane. But thank you for defending my honor," I tease. He winks at me and hands me a plate.

Will and I take sandwiches into the living room where Jeremy is just getting off the phone. "Did you hear about Steve?" he asks.

"No. What about him?" Will asks in response, handing Jeremy a plate.

"Who's Steve?" I ask at the same time.

"He was a PI who worked for my dad. He got killed last night, just a little while after Luke's dad, apparently. I wonder if their murders were related," Jeremy explains.

Well, if Steve went by Big_Dick_73, they were. And from the sound of it, I believe that's the case. Fuck. How did I not realize that my guys are so close to all of this? I need to do more digging to make absolutely sure none of them are involved.

That's ridiculous. Of course, none of them are involved with the sex trafficking ring I've been slowly taking down. If they were, I would have already uncovered the connection. That thought doesn't stop me from tapping into their computers and double checking while Jeremy and Will discuss Steve and how great a guy he was.

I feel a little guilty for searching their computers, but when I find absolutely nothing that ties them to the ring, relief settles in my chest. And what's a little more guilt to go with what I'm already feeling for hurting Luke?

"Do the cops have any leads on either case?" I can't force myself to say the word 'murder' because that's not what these were.

"Nothing. There was no physical evidence at either scene. No evidence that ties them together, except that Steve worked for my dad, and Luke's dad was his banker. So, I guess the only connection is my dad," Jeremy explains. "Honestly, if I didn't know better, I would think they were both professional hits."

"Really?" I ask. Jeremy nods as he takes a bite of his sandwich. Fuck. I could be closer to getting caught than I realized. Oh, shit. This is bad.

Jeremy connecting Steve, his dad, and Luke's dad makes me wonder. What if Jeremy's dad is the one behind the ring? I'll have to do some research and see what I find. I doubt he'd be stupid enough to have the stuff on his personal computer, but stranger things have happened. If I'm lucky, he won't have anti-virus software and I'll be able to get in without a cam call being involved. Especially since he's seen me and could recognize me.

"I just found an article about Steve. Apparently, there was evidence at the scene that he's been involved with that big sex trafficking ring the cops have been trying to pin down," Will says, turning his phone so we can see the article.

This is an interesting development. I wonder if they'll connect the dots. "Wow," I respond, unsure of what else to say. I search their faces to gauge their reactions to this news.

"That's insane. How would he even get involved in something like that?" Jeremy asks.

"I don't know, but if that's what got him killed, I'd say he deserved it," Will says.

"Definitely," Jeremy agrees. "Do you think that Luke's dad—?" He doesn't finish the question, but now that the thought is out there, they both seem to consider it. I didn't know the man prior to all this, so I have no idea how he portrayed himself to the guys.

"Before today, I wouldn't think so. But it's possible, I guess. My dad is always getting weird messages and taking cryptic sounding calls when I'm around. I wouldn't put it past him, either. That's one of the reasons I refuse to work for him. I don't want to be involved in whatever he's got going on," Will explains.

"Same here. But my dad is more secretive about everything, not just his phone, so it's hard to tell what he's doing. He doesn't take calls in front of anyone or check messages. It's like everything is a high priority confidential case, and no one but him has clearance." Jeremy's statement makes me suspect his dad even more. Without proof, there's nothing I can do. I'll just have to bide my time and do some research.

"Do you guys really think your dads could be involved in something like that?" I ask, desperately searching my mind for some way to change the subject without alerting them to me being connected to everything.

Will shrugs, and Jeremy takes another bite of his sandwich. "It really wouldn't surprise me. I don't want to be connected to that, but I can't control my dad."

Jeremy looks at me intensely. "I wish I could say I'd be surprised, but after Mom left him, I know Dad went through some sick stuff. It was all in the name of 'finding himself' as he put it. He swore none of it was illegal, but who knows?"

I have no idea how to respond to that, so we sink into silence. I'm not sure if it's awkward or comfortable, but I can't say anything that could tip them off to my secret. After we finish our sandwiches, I decide to try changing the subject.

"I wonder how long Luke is going to sleep. He made me promise to stick around. I have things I need to do, but I don't want to leave when he needs me." It's not a lie, but guilt still pangs at me.

"I'm not sure, but if you need to go because of work, I know he'd understand," Will says, rubbing my arm.

I shake my head. "Work can wait. I won't leave Luke when he's this upset."

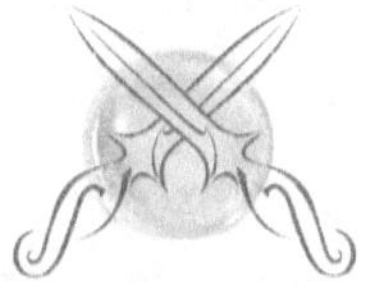

Luke ends up sleeping for three more hours before he finally emerges from his room. Jeremy, Will, and I are watching a movie when he walks in and sits on top of Will to get near me. "Hey, man. I love you, but you cannot sit on my lap!" Will objects and scoots over to make room for him. I know he's teasing, and Luke gives him a small smile.

"How are you feeling?" I ask, hoping that the nap helped at least as much as his tears did earlier. Luke rests his head on my shoulder and threads his fingers with mine.

"Eh," he says with a shrug. That tracks. I don't expect him to be feeling better yet. This is hard for him, and it's my fault. I have to do whatever I can to help him heal.

"What can I do?" Guilt burns in my chest again. Each breath feels like I'm fanning the flames. I feel as if I'll spontaneously combust at any moment. I have to make sure they don't catch on to my inner turmoil. So, I breathe normally, even though every breath hurts more than the last.

"Just be here," he answers quietly, turning his attention to the movie. Okay, I can be here. It's the very least I can do to make up for what I've taken from him; for the pain I've caused one of the men I'm falling for. Tears fill my eyes, and I fight to keep them from falling. If they see me cry, they'll feel bad for me. I don't deserve their sympathy.

This feeling is so much different from the usual melancholy that hits after a job. This is more akin to actual regret. I've never second guessed my job before. I am ridding the world of scumbags who deserve to die for what they do to young women and children. I can't feel bad for that. But this time, I do. Maybe I'm not cut out for this kind of work after all.

I can't help thinking that it's a little late for a career change, especially since I just accepted membership in the guild. This is their fault. I wouldn't have killed Luke's dad if not for their stupid contract with no loopholes. Fuck.

That's not fair, either. If I continued taking out members of this sex trafficking ring, there would have come a point where

I found out about Donovan on my own. And I would have taken him out anyway. I can't stop the guilt, but I can try to help Luke feel better, no matter how hard it is for me.

The movie plays, but my mind is elsewhere. I can't focus on anything but what I've done and what I still need to do. I reach out with digital tendrils to see what I can find online about Jeremy's dad and Will's dad. I need to know if they're connected to all this or not. No matter how badly I want them to be innocent, I can't get past the nagging feeling that they have just as much blood on their hands as Donovan did.

I should be at least a little upset about Steve, too. But until the guys showed me who he was, Steve was nothing but a random name on a screen. Even though I took his life for what I found on his computer, in addition to the contract that was taken out on him, he still wasn't real to me. Now he is. Steve had an ex-wife and two kids that he saw once a month. They're better off without him, but they don't know that. The kids are too young to understand that sentiment.

I wonder if I should have left some evidence of Donovan's role in all this for the cops or his family to find. I hate the thought that Luke might have seen it; that's what stopped me. I can't let that happen again. I have to do the job and separate that from personal ties.

I'm good at my job; it's my mission. I have to take this ring down, no matter who gets hurt in the crossfire. They have to be stopped. No matter what the personal cost is. Even if I lose everyone I love, I have to save these women and children who are being exploited. They're depending on me. It doesn't matter that they have no idea I exist. I'm the only one who can save them. I have to keep going. I can't let this speed bump stop me. But am I prepared to walk away from happiness if that's what it takes?

I have to be. Knowing it and doing it are two very different things. I'm not sure that when push comes to shove, I'll actually be able to leave. I hope I don't find out.

By the time the movie is over, Luke is asleep again, with his head resting on my lap. I don't have the heart to wake him up. "I can carry him to bed so you can head out," Jeremy offers.

"I don't want to wake him," I say.

"He won't wake up." Jeremy proves his point by hoisting Luke into his arms. My sweet vampire doesn't even seem to notice.

"I'll be back first thing in the morning," I insist, kissing Luke's forehead before pressing a kiss to Jeremy's lips. Will stops me at the door and kisses me.

"He'll be okay. We'll keep an eye on him tonight. Get some rest so you can recover, too." I'd nearly forgotten my excuse for avoiding them for two days.

"Yeah, I'm feeling pretty run down right now." It's not a lie, but I can't explain why I feel that way, either.

I head back down to my apartment, stopping to lean against the door after I close it. Tears stream down my face. I feel so loved and so alone at the same time. Each of my guys expressed concern about my health today, making the guilt over lying to them worse.

I have to figure out how to handle this before I end up doing something stupid and confessing. There's no way to finish what I've started from behind bars, and I don't want to give up what I have with the guys. I hate myself for being so selfish, but I can't help it. I've been through so much in my life already.

GUILT AND PENNANCE

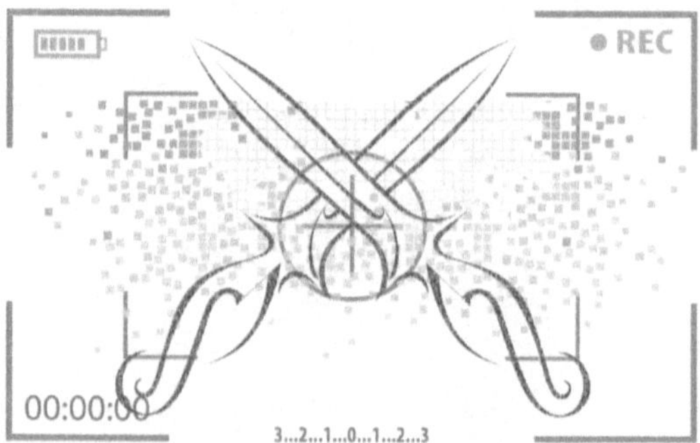

EMILY

Once I'm back in my apartment, I wish I hadn't promised to go back upstairs in the morning. I don't know how I can keep facing them when I'm the one who's caused their misery. But I know I can't stay away from them either. No matter how dangerous it is to be around them.

How long will it be until they figure that out and either turn me in, kill me, or worse, tell me to get lost? It has to say something about my mental state if I think being sent away is worse than death, but I don't focus on that. I can't, or I'll have to admit how real my feelings for them are.

I go through the motions with my cam clients. I don't really enjoy it like I used to. Transforming myself from Emily to Jasmin used to be fun, like playing dress up, or acting in a play. It's just not the same now, and I'm not sure exactly why. This experience seems to be changing me—but which experience? If I'm honest with myself, I've felt off about everything since I started falling for the guys.

I can't just disappear from my cam life, though. I need to keep my clients happy so that I can continue to use this as a cover for my other job. The job that's never made me feel guilty before, and I don't know how to deal with it.

It's weird how much everything feels different since I agreed to commit to my guys. And none of it is because of them. The timing of it all is eerie, though. Is the universe trying to tell me I can't be happy? I hope not, because I don't want to give these guys up. I can't.

After a fitful night's sleep, I head to the coffee shop around the corner to grab breakfast. If I'm ever going to make it up to the guys, I have to start somewhere. Coffee and donuts sound like as good a place as any. With my arms loaded down with bags of pastries and a drink carrier, I head up to their apartment.

Jeremy answers after one knock, and I know they've had as little sleep as I have. "Was it bad?" I ask, handing over part of my haul.

He nods, letting me walk ahead of him into the kitchen. "Luke is having nightmares now. They started shortly after you left. Somehow, he got the idea that whoever killed his dad is coming after him next."

"What? That's ridiculous," I say, stopping myself from finishing my thought. I would never take Luke out the way I did his father. I can't tell them that, though. Admitting what I've done would ruin everything. "Why would anyone want to hurt Luke?"

"That's what we've been trying to convince him—that no one is after him. Sadly, that doesn't stop the nightmares," Jeremy explains, pulling me into a hug after we set everything on the table.

"I just got him back to sleep," Will says as he enters the room. "He'll have to drink cold coffee later, because I'm not going back in there to wake him, and neither are you." The forcefulness in Will's voice makes my heart jump. I'm happy that they're all so protective of each other. I guess growing up together will do that for people, though.

I hand each of them a cup, then pick up a bag of pastries with mine and head to the living room. They only ever eat dinner in the kitchen, so I know I'm not overstepping. Will and Jeremy follow me, taking seats beside me on the couch. While I enjoy their warmth, I also feel a little smothered because of everything going on inside my head right now.

We eat in silence, drinking our hot coffee between bites of sugary goodness. Part of me is dying to ask more about their families, to learn more about their fathers, but I'm too scared to ask. What used to be comfortable silence is filled with anticipation, and not in a good way. Jeremy and Will don't seem to notice that I'm distracted at first.

"Em?" Exasperation is clear in his voice, and I'm certain it's not the first time Will's said my name. His hand waves in front of my face, and my cheeks turn red.

"I'm sorry, I guess I was daydreaming. What is it?" I shake myself to refocus.

"I asked if you were going to stick around today, or if you had to work," Jeremy responds. Fuck. I hadn't thought past breakfast.

"I have to work, but I can come back after if you want," I offer. As much as I enjoy spending time with them, I'm paranoid that I'm somehow going to let it slip that I'm the one responsible for all of this. I can't give myself that chance. I need to find a way to prevent that from happening.

"I'm sure there are rules and stuff about your job, but can you tell us anything about your clients? We've only seen your public show, so we're curious about the private chats," Will interjects.

"You're right, I can't tell you much, but," I respond, pausing for dramatic effect, "I pretty much do whatever my clients ask me to. Within reason, and as long as they're paying."

Both men's eyes go wide. I can see their imaginations going wild with crazy ideas about what I do for money. I expect to see judgement from them, but it doesn't happen.

"That's awesome. But you have control, right? No one can force you to do something you're not comfortable with, can they?" Jeremy asks.

They scoot as close to me as possible and each of them takes one of my hands. I can feel their concern through our connection.

I smile, shaking my head. "No one can make me do anything. They ask, and I decide if I'm willing or not. Sometimes, it depends on what they'll pay. Other times, it's a simple yes or no. There are a few things I've done on cam that are not my favorite, but I was paid well, so I agreed. But all of it is consensual."

I don't want to get into details about my cam calls, so I try to change the subject. "Most of what I have to do today is for subscribers in the general channel, though. I don't have too many private appointments."

"That means we'll get to watch," Will says, high-fiving Jeremy in front of me. Fuck. I'm not prepared to perform knowing that they're part of my audience. I knew that they'd seen my streams, but didn't realize that meant they were subscribers.

"What? You guys subscribed? That's crazy, especially after you figured out it's me." I try my best to sound convincing instead of intimidated.

"To be fair, we subbed before we knew it was you. But just because we know you, that doesn't mean we can't support you. Besides, the shows are hot." Jeremy makes a good argument, but I'm still a little uncomfortable.

"I just meant you didn't have to waste your money, that's all." I voice my concern without considering that they have the extra money to spend.

"Nothing to do with you is a waste of money," Will replies. It's a sweet sentiment, and I appreciate what he's saying. I still feel awkward knowing that they're watching streams. And paying for it, when they could be getting their own private shows for free.

"I guess we'll just have to agree to disagree, then." I finish my donut and coffee, then settle back between them. I could stay until lunch, but I need to do some thinking and prepare for my stream. Luke is still sleeping when I stand up to leave.

"You're coming back for lunch, right? Luke will be pissed at us for not waking him up if you don't," Jeremy says. It's a guilt trip and he knows it. I can't help feeling like I deserve it, though.

"Of course. I'll be back around one. What do you want me to pick up for lunch?" I shouldn't ask, but I can't help it. I have to find a way to make this mess up to them.

"You're not buying us lunch. You got breakfast, so one of us will take care of lunch," Will insists. I can't argue with his reasoning, so I agree. After we say goodbye, I race down to my apartment.

Once inside, I lock the door and slide down the wall next to it. I have no idea how long I sit there, staring into the apartment. From this vantage point, I feel like an outsider looking in on my life. I'm surprised that Will didn't comment on my lack of furniture when he was here.

It's not something I ever really needed before. But if this four-person relationship is gonna work, I'll have to let them into my apartment sometimes. And that will require places to sit at least. It's not like I can just have them over for sex all the time. At some point, they'll want to hang out.

I don't know why I'm so hesitant to fully commit to a relationship with them. Even if it's unconventional, it makes us happy. That's the important part. I mean, yeah, my secret life is a consideration. As long as I can maintain my own space, that shouldn't be a problem. Daydreaming isn't getting me anywhere, so I pick myself up and head to my cam room.

Instantly, a sense of calm washes over me. Being this close to my computer set up relaxes me and eases my mind. I reach out with my power and check my schedule. I have a stream and one call later. I'm experimenting with stream content, so I run through my song choices. After making my selection, I go over the moves I'll make to the music, doing a practice run of the dance routine I plan to start with.

Having that taken care of, I walk to the closet and open it. I have to select an outfit and want something that will accentuate my performance while giving me something to take off slowly. Am I spending way more time on this than usual? Yes. Does that have anything to do with the three men I know will be watching? I'd rather not answer that question, thank you very much.

I hate to think that they're changing me, but I know it's true. Camming used to be something I didn't put a lot of thought into. I just logged on and did what felt right, or what people asked for. Since my guys discovered my secret, I have to admit, I've been putting a little more time into planning things for the streams. My fans seem to appreciate it, and I'm getting bigger tips, so I guess it's working out.

Settling on a cutout bodysuit with a lacy babydoll over top, I head to the bathroom to shower. While I'm under the steaming spray, I forget for a moment, everything that's going wrong in my life. I think about Luke, Will, and Jeremy watching my live stream, and I get excited. Thinking about them makes me remember the other night, when we were all together.

I lather up my hands and run them over my body. A shiver runs up my spine, and I pause for a moment with my breasts in my hands. I can picture Jeremy and Will teasing my nipples while Luke lapped at my entrance. I roll my nipples between my fingers, then slide a hand down my stomach. My fingers stroke at my clit for a second before dipping inside me. I mimic the motions Luke made that night with his tongue, building myself up to my release.

When I come, I cry out their names. Maybe I should head upstairs a little early so there's time for a quickie before lunch. Then I can be sure I won't be late to the live stream. I push the thought away as soon as I have it. Sex isn't what Luke needs right now.

I take my time washing up, then wash and condition my hair. Turning off the water, I grab a towel and dry myself before stepping out and wrapping it around me. I wrap my hair in an old t-shirt, then head back to my bedroom to get dressed. A quick check of the time tells me that I haven't drawn everything out as much as I'd hoped.

I have nothing to do for a couple of hours. I could head back upstairs already, but I'm still worried that I'll slip up and say the wrong thing. Or I'll end up talking them into an orgy that Luke's not really up for. Since I don't want either of those things to happen, I decide that maybe a nap is the best option.

After setting an alarm, I drop the towel and t-shirt on the floor and climb into bed. I stare at the ceiling, expecting to struggle with everything weighing on my mind. Within minutes, I'm fast asleep, lost in dreams of my past mixed with my fears of the future.

Luke's father merges with the man my father sold me to, and in my dreams, I'm the one who kills him. With my hand still in his chest, my father's voice echoes around me. "Good job," he says. "And to think, I tried to sell you because I thought you were worthless."

I turn toward him and rip his heart out again. This time, I know exactly what I'm doing, and I don't freak out after. Of course, I'm not that child anymore. As his body collapses, my father stabs me with a knife I didn't see.

I wake with a start, clutching my stomach and expecting to see a blade sticking out of my gut. There's nothing, though, and I scrub my hands over my face, wiping away tears I hadn't realized were falling. I flop back on the bed, giving myself a minute to calm my racing heart. I stare at the ceiling as I focus on each thud in my chest, willing the rhythm to slow down.

Deep breath in, hold; out slow. It takes a few minutes, and I have to check my stomach again to make sure that I didn't really get stabbed. Once my brain finally comprehends that it was a dream, my heart rate slows and I can finally think again. As worried as I am about my secret coming out, I'm more upset by the dream. I make a quick post about a sudden emergency I need to deal with and cancel my stream for today, sending a short message to my call client as well. I won't be at my best after that nightmare.

I dress quickly and head upstairs. I'll be early for lunch, but it won't matter. The guys have never turned me away before, and I don't expect them to do so now.

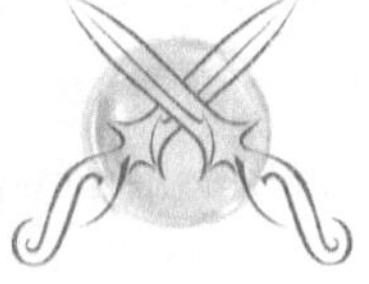

LUKE

When I hear the quiet knock at the door, somehow, I know it's Emily. I'm not handling my father's murder very well. I haven't left my room all day. Will and Jer have been great about making sure I'm not alone, but it's not their responsibility to take care of me.

I dash to the door, bumping Jer out of the way, and throwing it open to drag Em into my arms. She's been crying, and I wonder if she'll tell us why.

"Hey, you. How are you feeling today?" she asks with a small smile.

"Much better with you here. How about you?" I tip her head up so she has to look at me. I can tell she doesn't want to answer, and I'm sure she knows I won't push.

"Nightmares again; bad enough to cancel my stream today, but I'm okay. Nothing to worry about. I just need some company, and I wanted to check on you," she whispers.

I don't want to admit that I love the way she clings to me. I hate that she has nightmares, and even more that she doesn't want to tell us what they're about. Her parents died when she was younger, and I'm sure that has something to do with it. More than anything, I want to chase the monsters that haunt her away.

I scoop her up and dash back to the couch, dropping onto the soft cushions with her on my lap. Jer grumbles as he shuts the door and follows us. I chuckle when he flops onto the chair across from us.

"Well, you took care of me yesterday when I needed you. So, today it's my turn. What can I do to make you feel better?"

Something akin to guilt crosses Em's features, and I would swear that my kitten was keeping secrets. But what could she possibly have to hide from us? Besides her cam girl persona, that is. Since we already know about that, I'm guessing this is something else. If it's important, she'll tell us.

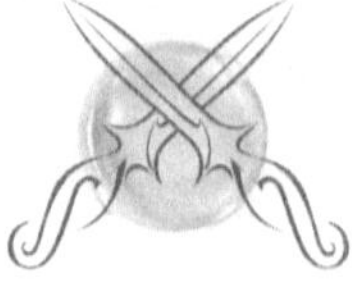

EMILY

Luke's desire to care for me is touching. It definitely makes my guilt flare, though, and I can see in his eyes that he's noticed something. All I can do is hope he doesn't ask. "You really don't have to do that. Let me take care of you. This week has been tough, and you deserve a break."

He shakes his head and hugs me tighter. I look to Jeremy for assistance, but he's frowning at his phone and not paying any attention to us. I wiggle a bit, acting like I'm trying to get away from Luke. I know I can't, and I don't want to anyway. I'm certain he knows it, but he plays along.

"Where's Will?" I ask, realizing that he's not here.

"His dad called and he had to go home for a while. Dave is freaked out about what happened to my dad. He thinks that Will being here will put a target on his back next. As if it's all connected to me somehow," Luke says quietly. I've hit a nerve without meaning to.

"I'm sure that's not true, even if it's what his dad thinks." My reassurance does nothing to change Luke's expression.

"We've all told him that; but he doesn't want to believe us," Jeremy chimes in. It seems as if he was paying attention to our conversation after all.

"Look, I know it's paranoid. What if it's true? What if I'm putting all of you in danger because some rogue vampire hunter is out there targeting us?" Luke's forehead glistens with sweat and he starts to shake.

"What makes you think it's a vampire hunter? The other guy who was killed wasn't a vamp, was he? It seems to me like there's more of a chance that it was some kind of business they were both involved in than a racial thing." I almost slip up and tell him exactly why his father and the other guy were killed, but I stop myself.

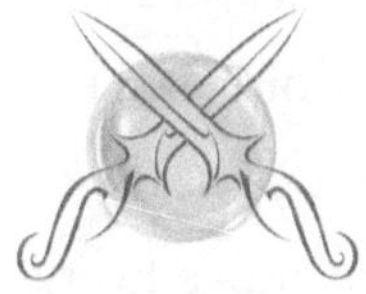

WILL

Being summoned by my father is not my idea of a good time. I walk into his office, nodding at his secretary as I pass her desk. I try not to notice her short skirt or the amount of cleavage showing from her low-cut top. It's no wonder Mom thinks he's cheating.

"What's this all about?" I snap when the door closes behind me. He jumps at my voice, and I notice that he's taking care to keep his phone covered. That's weird, but I have no idea why.

"Will, I'm glad you came," my father answers, setting his phone face down on the desk.

"I didn't have much choice. You made that pretty clear. What is going on? You call me and claim I'm being threatened because I live with Luke. That's ridiculous." I don't want to have this argument again, but I will not let my father bully me into moving home. I like my apartment and my roommates.

"You *need* to come home, son. It's not safe living with those boys. Your mother is worried about you. If I'm honest, I am too."

I shake my head and close my eyes. "No."

"What do you mean, 'no.' You will pack your things and come home today. Or I will cut off your access to the family money. Do I make myself clear?" A vein in Dave Jeffries' neck pulses. I'm pissing him off, and I don't care.

"*Crystal.* But I'm not doing it. I have my own bank account, and I make my own money. I don't even spend yours anymore. So, no, *Father*, I will not move home because you demanded it. Is there anything else you needed to waste my time with? I have a friend who's just suffered a tragic loss and needs me." I hope that Luke is feeling better today. He was still locked in his room when I left, and I haven't gotten to talk to him yet. Other than comforting him while he struggled with his nightmares last night.

"You can't be serious," he scoffs.

"I can assure you, sir, that I am serious. Cut me off. Disown me. *I don't care.* I'm not your puppet, and I won't be jerked around by you anymore. I'm a grown man, and I have my own life to live. If you don't like it, you can *fuck off*," I growl. It's not smart, and I know it. My father has a temper, and it has a very short fuse.

He's around the desk with his hand on my throat before I can move. "I gave you everything, and this is how you talk to me? I should snap your neck right now, you disrespectful little shit."

For a second, I think he's going to do it. But he hesitates, and that's all the opening I need. I punch him in the gut, then the jaw, and he releases me. Coughing and sputtering, I draw in a few ragged breaths. I back up to the door, putting space between us.

"I might be a disrespectful little shit, but at least I'm not abusive. This is the last time you'll ever put your hands on me. If you try again, I will kill you. Do you understand me, old man?" I lock eyes with him and for a moment, I think he might be scared. It's hard to tell, because he's a shapeshifter like me. We have an easy time bluffing, because we can change our eyes at will.

"You don't know what you're doing. Come home now and I'll forgive this transgression," he offers. I shake my head and laugh at him.

"Why do you want me home so badly? You'll never be able to control me the way you do Mom. You might as well forget it, because I'm never coming back now," I say, jerking the door open and storming out.

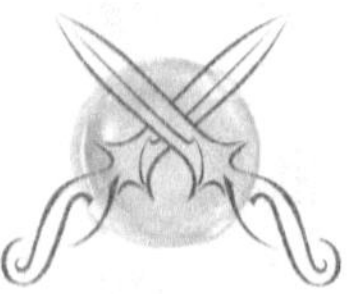

EMILY

The door slams and I turn to see Will storming into the apartment. I stand up and walk toward him. "Are you okay? Luke said your dad called and you had to go meet him."

Will shakes his head but lets me pull him into my arms. He's so upset that he's shaking. Once he's in my arms, he hugs me so tight that it's hard to breathe. I won't complain, though. He needs me, and I'll do whatever I can to make him feel better.

Luke and Jeremy walk over and wrap their arms around us. The group hug is nice, even if I'm being squished. "What did he say this time?" Jeremy asks.

"The usual. I need to move home. This time he told me that he's cutting me off." Will coughs a little, and I notice the purple marks on his neck.

"Did he do this to you?" I ask, my eyes going wide. Rage boils through me, and I desperately want to be the one to handle his father.

Will blushes and dips his head. "It's okay, really. I punched him a couple of times, and he knows now that he'll never touch me again. Or else."

"Damn straight," I mutter. I find myself wishing that Will's dad had been my target instead of Luke's.

"I'm sorry that your dad treated you that way," Luke says. "It was because of what happened to my dad, wasn't it?"

"Don't worry about it, Luke. I took care of it. I'm not going anywhere, and he understands that now." Will hugs Luke, looking at me over his shoulder. It's touching how close these guys are, and I'm thrilled to be part of it.

Even as I have the thought, I know that this drama is my fault. If I hadn't accepted the contract and killed Luke's father...no, that's not fair. He would have been taken out anyway, even if it had been someone else who did it.

I've worked most of my life to rid the world of these horrible men. I can't let myself second guess that now. I have to keep researching the trafficking ring and find out who's in charge. If I can take him or her out, I might be able to stop them all. I have to stay focused on the mission and stop letting guilt tear me apart.

"I'll get lunch started," Jeremy offers, heading to the kitchen. A few minutes later, we're all settled on the couch with plates full of sandwiches and pasta salad.

Will turns on a movie, and we eat in silence. For the first time in days, it actually feels comfortable instead of awkward.

THE NEXT MARK

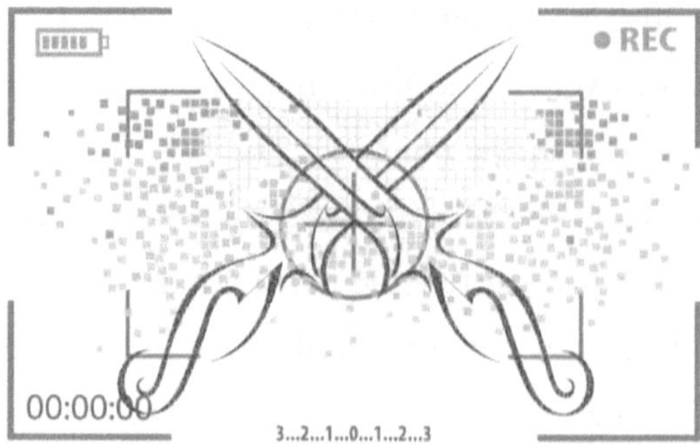

EMILY

Spending time with my guys is just what I need to chase the aftermath of my nightmare away. By the time we finish the movie, my spirits are lifted. They tease me about canceling my cam show this afternoon, and I roll my eyes.

"Go ahead and make fun...I can always terminate your subscriptions so you can't watch anymore," I threaten with a laugh.

As their objections ring out, something small and hot pink catches my eye from the console table against the wall. The small orb seems to be calling to me. I dart over and pick it up, knowing instantly what it is.

"Hey, what's that?" Will asks, walking toward me.

"Nothing," I say, squeezing the orb in my palm. It pops and absorbs into my hand, sending the next target information straight to my brain.

I open my hands, showing Will that I don't have anything as I try to process the fact that my next job is Mr. Jeffries.

I need to talk to Brynn about their job delivery system. This is getting a little too close for comfort. I can't let my guys find out about my other job. Not like this. There may come a time when we can talk about it and they might understand, but this is not the time. I can't imagine it will be a comfortable conversation anyway, but Will discovering that I'm an assassin because I just accepted a job to kill his father? No thanks.

This particular mark will be an even bigger challenge. Will and Jeremy's fathers have met me; they know what I look like. I won't be able to gain access through camming. Fuck. How am I going to do this? There's only one way that it will work.

"Did you really cancel your stream today?" Luke asks. I nod in response.

"Do you want to talk about why?" Will presses. I shake my head.

"Actually, I'm feeling a lot better. I think I might be able to do the show after all." The lie is bitter on my tongue, but I push on. I have a job to do, and I can't let my guilt or other feelings get in the way. "What time is it? I left my phone in my apartment when I came up here."

He pulls his phone out and checks the time, turning it so I can see. "You've got time. We won't let you be late, if you're going to do your cam show at the usual time."

I wrap my arms around him, hugging his arms to his sides so he can't put the phone away yet. I need to tap into it and find a path to his father so that I can get to him later. "Thank you. You guys are so sweet to me. I don't deserve it." The hug lasts long enough to make things awkward, but I find the path and mark it so I'll find it later.

When I let go, Will stares at me for a minute. "I think we don't deserve you, so I guess we're even." Guilt eats at me over his sweet words, and I almost confess my darkest secret.

I give him a quick kiss, then walk back to the couch and kiss Luke and Jeremy. "I have to get ready for the stream. You guys are still gonna watch, right?" Suddenly I'm nervous that they won't tune in for some reason. Maybe it's knowing that I've already betrayed them, and I'm about to do it again. Maybe it's general insecurity that goes along with dating. I have no idea. I can't waste time worrying about it either.

"Of course, we are," Luke reassures me. "Just not together."

"Because watching together would be weird?" I ask, cocking an eyebrow.

Jeremy shakes his head. "No, because we wouldn't all be able to tip you if we watched together." He says it as if it's the simplest explanation, and they've discussed the different options for watching before. I'm not sure if that makes it better or worse.

"Strangely, that makes sense. I'll see you guys later." They each kiss me again, and I practically float downstairs from the euphoria of it. I carry that feeling with me for a while longer as I get dressed and set everything up for the cam show. My nerves have settled, and I'm more excited to perform for my guys than anxious that they'll be watching. As I get dressed and do my make up, I post a message letting my subscribers know that the emergency has been dealt with and the show will go on. My call client has already rescheduled, so I'll leave that alone.

I go over the routine in my head again, making sure I have the timing figured out. For today's performance, I select an orange wig to match the babydoll I'm wearing. Once it's in place, I check the mirror to make sure I look as good as I feel. I start my play list at the same time as the camera, making sure that I'm not in frame yet.

I've been starting the stream a minute before I make my entrance lately, and it seems to work better for me. Today, I'm not doing my usual intro, though. I'm starting with my dance, then I'll talk to my subs and take a couple of requests.

The song I selected earlier starts to play, and I weave my way around the room, going through the motions I'd practiced before. I use my power to keep the camera focused on me, and make sure that I stay in the studio area of the room. I feel sexy and powerful, exactly the way I want. With this routine, I become Jasmin—fearless and in control.

When the song ends, I take my place on the edge of the bed and address my viewers. I know there are nearly a thousand of them watching me right now, and several are sending tips in addition to their monthly subscription fees. I try not to react to the larger tips that come through, making sure to thank my benefactors for their generosity without calling them out in detail.

"Thank you all for joining me today." I settle into my chat segment, allowing my viewers to make requests for me to act out.

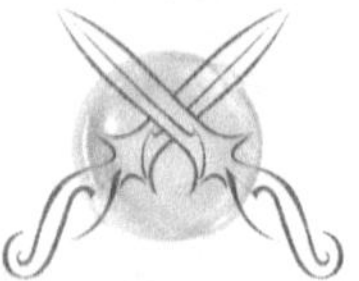

When the live stream ends, I have texts waiting from each of my guys. I shut down the camming system while I read them all.

> *You looked so sexy tonight.*

Luke's sweet comment stabs me right in the feels.

> *Was all that just for us, sugarplum?*

My cheeks heat as they flush at Will's message.

> *Damn, Em. That was hot.*

Jeremy's text makes me laugh out loud.

I respond to each of them, then decide that I might as well get back to work. Will's dad isn't likely to kill himself, so I need to figure out exactly how I'm going to deal with that. I've never been to Jeffries' house, and I can't exactly cam call him to see the layout. I'll be going in blind on this one, and I'm not excited about it.

I have to admit, there is a certain rush of adrenaline at knowing that this job could be the one that gets me caught. It won't be, because I'm better than that. It's probably a good idea to check the house out and get schematics if I can. I need to at least know where the entrances and exits are.

I slip into my secret room, locking the hidden door behind me. I don't expect my guys to show up, but if they manage to get inside before I return, I need to make sure this space is protected. Once I'm safely inside the walls, I shift into my pixelated form and slide into my computer.

Traveling along network lines is a thrill in itself. With outages coming randomly, I never know if I'll get stuck somewhere and have to find another way back. That's only happened a few times, though, and it prepared me for what to do in those cases. Things like that are the reason my back up plans have back up plans.

When I get to Jeffries' house, I don't leave the computer. Instead, I go through every file on it, looking for the proof I need to be certain this is one of the traffickers. What I find is worse than I ever expected. Not only is he involved; he's one of the top parties controlling the ring. There are records proving that he purchased his wife the day she turned eighteen. I feel awful for Will, and even worse for his mom. She deserves so much better than this.

As if that wasn't bad enough, the sex tapes he's made with her and other women are repulsive. To be fair, it's not that his kinks are so bad. The problem is that the women clearly are not into it, and he seems to enjoy forcing them way too much. After half a dozen videos, I stop myself from watching more.

There are hundreds of videos, but no way to know, short of watching them all, if Jeffries is the star of all of them or not. Since I don't have time for that, and I have enough proof now, I simply copy the files and send them to my encrypted account.

I still have to decide if I'm going to release everything to the press, or just the police. I don't want to put Luke or Will through any more than I absolutely have to. I wish I could talk to them about this and see what they want to do. But that would mean outing myself as an assassin and taking the chance that they might turn me in. I can't do that.

I search the internet for schematics of the house. When I find what I'm looking for, I inspect them carefully. I memorize the layout of the entire house, though calling this massive building a house is an understatement. It's a mansion, bordering on a castle.

I can't resist checking Jeffries' bank accounts. The man has more money than I do. And that's saying something, because I've skimmed off the top of everyone I've ever killed. I work my magic, moving some of his money around. As long as I do it just right, no one will ever know it wasn't him.

Once I've redistributed his wealth, I feel pretty confident that I can take him out. With all the damning evidence I found, I don't want to wait. I can't give him a chance to be harder to find. I got Jeffries' cell number from Will's phone, so I can easily locate him in the giant house. It's late enough that no one else should be here, except his wife. I should probably check the house for other cell phone signals, but I want this done.

Even if someone is here, I just need to corner him and finish my mission. That won't be too hard. I follow the phone's signal to the room Jeffries is in. I'm anxious to complete this job, and it's making me sloppy. I have to refocus and do this right. This man cannot be the reason I get caught.

I climb out of the computer, looking around to make sure the room is empty. I decide it's safer to remain in my digital form, so I can't be seen by cameras or the security system. I have to work quickly so I can take Jeffries out and get home before anyone misses me.

I move through the house carefully. Even though I can't be seen, that doesn't mean it's safe to be in the open. I know from experience how easy it is to kill someone accidentally when I'm in this form. I'm only after my target; no one else needs to get hurt here.

I find Jeffries alone in the kitchen. This will be easy enough. Pausing for a moment to listen, I can hear someone in the bathroom down the hall, but I think I have enough time to do this. Normally, I would debate exactly how I wanted to kill him. At this moment, I don't have that luxury. I want the job done, so I have to improvise. I float up to him as he stirs his mug. From the smell, it seems to be some sort of tea blend.

Not wasting time on hesitations, I shove my hand into his chest. I watch as he realizes that something is wrong. Jeffries clutches his chest, his hand sliding through my arm. I wrap my fingers around his heart and squeeze. If I'm careful, this will look like a heart attack, and his murder won't be connected to the others.

I open my hand, releasing his heart. The relief on his face ignites anger inside me. I grip his heart again, squeezing and twisting. I want to rip it from his chest. But I have to be smart about this. I take a deep breath and center myself. I can't let my emotions get in the way.

I want this man dead for more than one reason. I know killing him is going to hurt Will on some level, and I hate that. At the same time, he deserves this for what he did to all those women, and for the way he treats his son. I don't let go of his heart until he starts to fall forward. Standing over his lifeless body, a sense of pride comes over me.

I turn to leave and almost run into Jeremy. "Dave?" Jeremy rushes past me; I barely have time to move so he doesn't go through me. I know he doesn't see me, but he sniffs the air.

"Emily?" he asks, turning to face me. I'm so startled that I almost drop my shift. How does Jeremy know I'm here? I don't have time to waste trying to figure it out.

He bends down and checks Jeffries for a pulse, then pulls his cell phone out of his pocket and dials it. I slip into the phone and disappear along the data lines that connect it to the internet.

Fuck, that was close. What was Jeremy doing there?

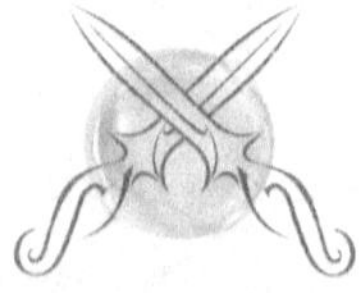

JEREMY

When I step into the kitchen and see Dave's body on the floor, I'm shocked. His hand is gripping his chest, so he must have had a heart attack. When I dash over to him, I swear I smell Emily. How is that possible? She can't be here. She doesn't even know where Will's dad lives.

I check him for a pulse, then call Will. "You need to get to your dad's now. I'll explain when you get here." I don't bother to wait for him to respond. I hang up and dial emergency services. Within minutes, Will arrives, then the ambulance.

"What are you doing here?" he asks, meeting me in the kitchen. His eyes go wide at the sight of his father on the floor. "What did you do to my dad?"

"It's not like that, Will, and you know it. He called me because he knew he screwed up today when you went to see him. Dave asked me to come over so we could talk while your mom is out of town. He wanted me to talk to you. I went to the bathroom, and he was like this when I got back," I explain. I pull him into my arms and hug him when his tears start to fall. I know they had a rocky relationship, but Dave was his dad, and Will loved him.

I want to tell him about the Emily thing, but I can't explain it. Maybe her perfume is on my jacket and I caught a whiff of it.

It's not like she was here. That's not possible. If she had been, I would have seen her. Right? I shake the thought away.

I have to focus and answer the EMT's questions. Since it looks like a heart attack, they'll run some blood tests to check for poisons and examine his body before deciding on the cause of death.

I'd hoped that something could be done to save him, but he was gone before I walked into the room. I can't get past the idea that Emily had been there. I can't figure out how she could get into the house and back out again without being seen. Will reviews the security system videos, giving me an alibi, and even more so when the video clearly shows Dave was alone when he died.

"That looks pretty clear to us. We'll still run some panels to be sure he wasn't poisoned. But for now, we'll call it natural causes," one of the EMTs says as they strap Dave to the gurney and prepare to wheel him out.

After they leave, Will and I lock up and head home. "Do you want to call your mom?" I ask as we walk to our cars.

He shakes his head. "No, I think I'll let the coroner or whoever at the hospital take care of that. I don't know what I would say to her."

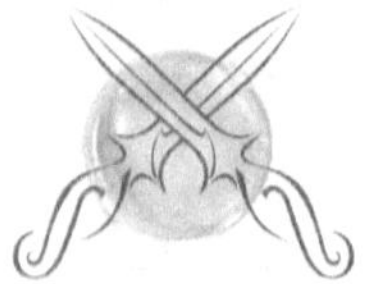

EMILY

I collapse onto my bed, my heart still racing from nearly being caught. Guilt swirls in my head as I check Jeremy's phone. He called Will after I left, then an ambulance. Fuck. I don't know if that means I'm safe or not.

I want to reach out and make sure Will is okay, but I can't do that without revealing my secret. I decide to let the thought go for now. Waiting is hard, but giving my secret away could be devastating. I don't want to go to jail. More than that, I don't want to see the pain and hurt in my guys' eyes when they realize that I've been lying to them.

That thought hurts me, even if the lying was to protect them. I can't let anyone think they were involved. If Jeremy somehow knows I was there, and turns me in, I'll take the full blame. I'll probably turn myself in if he hints at it. I have to protect them, no matter what it costs me. I strip down and step into my shower, turning the water as hot as it will go. I'll melt these feelings away if I have to.

With my fears taking hold of my imagination, I set up a trust that will go to the guys if I go to jail or if anything happens to me. The whole thing is anonymous, so none of the money can be traced to my unsavory activities.

I sit on the floor of my shower as scalding water washes over me. I've always been good at multi-tasking, but this seems to be taking things to extremes. After settling my finances and getting things squared away for the worst-case scenario, I lean back against the shower wall.

Water drips down my face, mingling with the tears I can't stop. I feel as if I'm on the verge of losing everything. Panic grips my heart. Can I go on with my life if Luke, Will, and Jeremy aren't in it? Probably. Do I want to? Not at all.

I scrub the tears from my face and turn the water off. Staring at myself in the mirror, I realize just how much blood is on my hands. I don't feel guilty about the lives I've taken. I feel guilty that I put my guys in the middle of my work. If I'm honest with myself, I know that's not true. Their fathers put them in my work. At least none of them are involved in the trafficking ring, so I don't have to worry about them becoming a target.

I dry myself slowly, trying to process everything that's happened today. I can't keep this up. I need to either cut ties with the guys or come clean about my secrets. I'm not sure which is the better choice. And I know that after tonight, I won't have time to consider those options for at least a few days.

As much as Luke wanted me around after his father's death, I'm certain Will isn't going to let me out of his sight once he gets to me. I throw on some comfy clothes and settle back on my bed to wait. I know I won't get sleep for a while with everything racing through my brain.

I answer the phone on the first ring, certain it's Will. "Sugarplum, I need you." The sadness in his voice rips me apart. It takes me a minute to remember that I shouldn't know what happened yet.

"What's wrong, Will?" I don't have to pretend to be concerned for him. But I do have to remember that I need to keep my secret if I can.

"My dad died tonight," he says, his voice barely a whisper.

"Oh, no! What happened?"

"They said it looks like a heart attack. Blood work should confirm that or prove it was murder." He pauses then continues, "Jeremy was with him. Apparently, it happened when he went to the bathroom. He found Dad when he came back but it was too late."

I mute the phone and breathe a sigh of relief. It sounds like Jeremy didn't say anything about sensing me. I still haven't figured out how he knew I was there. No matter how much I want to know, I'm not about to ask him.

"Are you home? I'll come up," I offer.

"I just walked in the door. Jeremy went to get food." Will pauses again, and I'm sure he's crying.

"I'll be right there," I say, hanging up the phone and grabbing my shoes. I don't bother to put them on but carry them with me as I race up the stairs. I'm tempted to shift so I can get there faster, but I don't want anyone to see me materialize, and I can't risk exposing myself to my guys like that.

The door opens before I can knock, and Will drags me into his arms. "Thank you." Guilt surges again, and I'm uncomfortable with being the person to comfort him for something I did. I drop my shoes beside the door and return his hug.

"Don't thank me. Being here for you is the least I can do," I insist. In my heart, I know the truth of my words. I could have refused the job. I could have ended the relationship. Being here is the very least I can do for any of them right now. If only I was stronger, then I could walk away.

My heart jumps inside of me as he holds me tightly. I'm in way too deep now to leave. I'm going to have to tell them everything. It's just a matter of timing now. Falling in love wasn't in my plans, but here I am, head over heels and unable to fight it.

I place my hands on Will's cheeks, forcing him to look at me. "I love you, Will." I kiss him gently, tenderly, reverently. I want him to understand that I mean everything with those words. Because soon, he'll have to decide if it's enough.

"I love you, sugarplum," he responds, pressing his lips to my forehead. I let my tears fall, mixing with his. There's no reason to hold back my emotions now. I need to soak up every moment before I ruin it all.

After a long moment, we head into the living room, where Luke waits for us. Will sits next to him, and I take the empty spot beside Will. My heart swells again when Luke threads his fingers through Will's and leans over to kiss my shapeshifter's cheek. There's nothing sexual about the contact, but it makes me wetter than I want to admit. I shouldn't be thinking about sex right now; not after what I've done.

I am a monster. I get off on killing sick and twisted men, then get turned on by watching their relatives pick up the pieces. I'm suddenly disgusted with myself. What kind of person does this to people they claim to love? I don't deserve to be here; I deserve to be locked up, or worse.

Luke and Will stare at me, and I wonder what kind of face I'm making. I relax my muscles, letting my expression go. "I'm so sorry. This sucks so bad. Both of you losing your dads like this. I wish I could fix it for you."

TRUTH COMES OUT

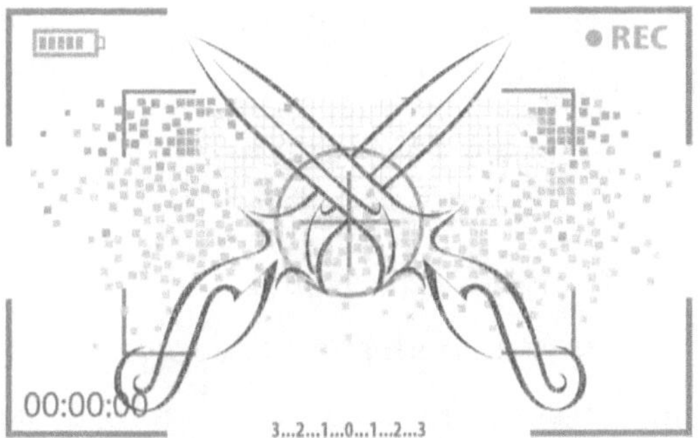

EMILY

The moment Jeremy walks into the apartment, I feel his eyes on me. Guilt surges again, and I don't think I can do this. I need to find out what gave me away, but I can't just ask him. I have to wait and see if he mentions it.

Luke darts over and grabs the bags of takeout from him. I do my best to act like usual, so I walk over and kiss him. He pins me to the wall and whispers in my ear, "We need to talk."

"About what?" I ask, knowing that my secret won't exist much longer. He locks eyes with me and stares.

"I think you know," he replies, too low for Will or Luke to hear unless they're actively trying to listen in. I can't speak because of the lump in my throat. I nod, trying to hold off the terror I'm feeling. He wraps his hand around my arm and drags me toward his room.

I glance at Will and Luke, who are standing in the living room staring at us. The looks on their faces tell me that they aren't sure if I need help or not. Honestly, I'm not sure if I need help or not. Jeremy shoves me into his bedroom and locks the door behind us.

"Jer, what's going on?" Will calls from the other side of the door.

"Hey, man, let us in," Luke insists.

Jeremy ignores them both and stalks toward me. Fury radiates off him in waves. I'm not sure how long he'll be able to hold off his shift, or if I'll survive when he does. Instinctually, I climb onto the bed and scoot toward the headboard.

"I have questions, and you're going to answer them honestly. Understand?" he growls at me as he paces back and forth beside the bed. I nod, too terrified to do anything else. Logically, I know that I am physically capable of taking him down if I had to, but I love this man, and can't imagine hurting him. I've accepted that if push came to shove, I would let him kill me instead of doing anything to defend myself against him.

"Was Will's dad one of your subscribers?"

"No," I whisper.

"Were you sleeping with him?"

"No." Some of my terror falls away. This is absolutely not the line of questioning I expected when he cornered me. "Did you lock us in here so you could ask me if I'm fucking someone else?"

"I'm asking the questions here. Don't forget that." He continues to pace, barely even glancing at me. "Why were you at Dave's house tonight?"

"What are you talking about? Why would you think I was there?" I try for indignation, but the best I can do is confusion. I seriously want to know but I'm still horrified at what his response could be.

Jeremy growls again, and his eyes flash yellow. I've never seen his wolf, but I'm certain he's barely holding back his shift. "I know you were there. I could smell you."

Fuck. I hadn't expected that. I was stupid and completely forgot about his heightened wolf senses. Of course, he'd be able to smell me even in my shifted form.

"Jeremy, I can explain." I pause and stare at him until he looks at me again. "You're not going to like it, though." I drop my head, fighting against the tears threatening to fall.

He stops mid-stride and stares back at me. "Well?"

"I should probably talk to all three of you at once," I explain, standing up and heading for the door. "Then if you want me to leave and never come back, I will." He steps out of my way so I can unlock the door and walk into the living room. I have to push past Will and Luke where they're trying to listen in.

The three of them follow me, taking seats next to each other on the couch. I kill people for a living, and yet, something about these three men staring at me is so much more intimidating. Taking a deep breath, I thread my fingers together and try to decide the best way to explain everything. I stand in front of the men I love, hoping I'm not about to destroy everything we have.

"There are things about me that you don't know. Please understand that I didn't keep them from you to hurt you, or because I'm ashamed. I have to keep my secrets, because otherwise, I'll go to jail or worse." Each man's expression is nearly identical. They're shocked and confused.

"I can't figure out an easy way to do this, so I'll just rip the bandage off. My cam girl persona was only one secret I hid. The reason I stream is that I use it as a cover for my main job." I can tell from changes in their expressions that now they're considering if I could be an undercover cop. Boy are they about to be disappointed.

"I'm an assassin. I kill people for money. And I'm good at it; or at least I was, until tonight," I pause as they start to sputter and try to ask questions. Holding up a hand, I continue, "I have a very strict code, and I only kill bad people. Specifically, I go after people involved in sex trafficking rings. These guys sell women and young girls to other people as sex slaves or worse, after kidnapping them from their lives and families."

"What the actual fuck?" Will asks. Jeremy fists his hands in his hair. Only Luke waits for me to continue, as if he knows that isn't the worst of it.

"There's more. I have proof for every single man I've killed that they were involved in sexual trafficking. I can show you, or I can send it all to the police. I'll leave that up to you guys. But you need to know the rest so you can decide if you ever want to see me again." I wait until they're settled before continuing.

"Please understand, I never meant to hurt any of you. But I did. Luke, I killed your father. And yours, Will. It's unforgivable, and I know that. I didn't want you to find out like this. I'm so sorry. I won't ask for forgiveness." I watch shock and horror cross their faces. When no one speaks, I turn to leave.

I don't know why I thought, even for a moment, that our relationship could survive this. What I've done is too horrific, too heartless, to ever warrant forgiveness. I walk out the door, not bothering to grab my shoes, wondering if they'll turn me in. Trudging slowly down the stairs, I consider my options.

I can stay and take my chances, or I can leave and start over somewhere else. I don't know what to do. I trust Jeremy, Luke, and Will with my life. I don't think they'd call the cops on me, but I can't assume that. It's not fair for me to ask them not to, either.

I lock myself in my apartment for the next two days. I spend my time in bed, in the shower, or where I am right now. Which is lying on the floor in the sparse living room staring at the ceiling, trying to decide if I should get furniture or pack what little I own, when a soft knock catches my attention. I reach out with my powers and find Will at my door.

Curiosity gets the better of me, and I open it. "Hi," he says shyly. It seems out of character, because usually Will is flirty and happy. I don't like seeing him upset. "Can I come in?"

I nod and open the door wider to let him inside. There's no one else in the hall, and I'm not exactly sure what this is all about. I didn't expect any of them to want to see me again after our last conversation.

"Look, I know that telling us your secret was hard. Thank you for trusting us. We're not gonna turn you in or anything. I've spent the last two days thinking about everything you said. Have you been following the news?" He gently grabs my hand and drags me toward my room.

We sit on the edge of the bed, but he doesn't let my hand go. "I haven't paid attention to much the past couple of days. Why?"

Will pulls out his phone and hits play on a video. A man is handcuffed and being walked into the police station with tons of paparazzi snapping pictures while people shout questions at him. The headline reads "Local Man Arrested in Connection with Sex Trafficking Ring."

"What is this?" I look at Will and he gives me a small smile.

"After our talk the other night, Jeremy went to see his dad. He didn't call first and caught his dad in the act. He stole a laptop from the house and turned him in. It looks like Lloyd Franklin was the head of the ring." Will pauses, staring into my eyes. "I can't say it makes me happy to know what you did, but I understand why you did it. Why you do it, I should say. And it won't be easy, but I'd really like another chance with you."

"Wait, what? I told you that I killed your dad, and you're asking *me* to give *you* another chance? Come on, Will, this is ridiculous. How can you ever want to be around me after what I've done?" Before he can answer, my bedroom door swings open. I jump, starting to freak out, until I realize that Jeremy and Luke let themselves in.

"Sorry, Em. We knocked, but you didn't answer. And the door was unlocked. We followed the voices," Luke says before I can respond to the surprise intrusion.

I feel tears streaming down my face. I've missed these three so much the past couple of days. But do they agree with Will? Can this really work out?

"Em, I know how hard this has been for you. I won't lie and say it isn't hard for us too, because knowing that the woman we love is an assassin; well, that's a lot to process. But we love you, Em. That doesn't just go away because you kept a secret from us." Jeremy's statement catches me off guard. I don't expect this kind of support from any of them.

Luke stands in front of me, taking my face in his hands. "I have to know something, though." He locks his eyes with mine and I know I'll answer any question he wants to ask, no matter how painful.

"Anything," I whisper.

"Why did you think you couldn't just tell us? I had no idea my dad was involved in all that. I'd have been the first one to turn him in if I had even suspected it. We do not condone the actions of our fathers. You have to know that," he says, pressing a kiss to my forehead.

"I didn't know how to tell you. Part of me thought I was protecting you; the rest was protecting me. I had no idea if you guys would turn me in or not. And honestly, I'm pretty good at what I do. It took someone familiar with my scent to figure me out," I respond.

"That's kind of what we figured. You have to promise us that you won't keep any more secrets. That's the only way this will actually work," Luke insists. I nod.

"I do have one more thing that I should tell you. Or maybe it's better if I show you," I say, standing up and stepping away from the three of them.

"More secrets?" Jeremy asks. Frustration is written all over his face.

"I like to think of it as more of an omission," I reply. He cocks an eyebrow at me, letting me know that he'll be the judge of that when he sees what I'm talking about. "This is something that no one knows about me. I've wanted to show you guys so many times, but I was scared."

Three sets of eyes stare at me as I stretch my hands out to my sides. Using my power, I turn the bedside lamp on. Then I shift into my pixelated form and float around the room.

"Where'd she go?" Luke asks.

"I'm right here," I answer, my voice a little distorted in this form.

"Wait, you turn invisible?" The awe in Will's question nearly floors me.

"Not exactly. I shift into pixels and can travel through computers and internet lines," I answer.

"I have to admit, that is not the secret I expected. Though it does explain why I didn't see you at Dave's," Jeremy says.

"We were face to face for a minute, and I thought somehow you'd seen me," I explain, floating near his ear. I move away from them again and shift back. "That's it. I have no other secrets."

"What about your childhood? You won't talk about it when we ask. Is that a secret, or just because of the trauma?" Luke asks. He sounds more curious than upset.

I take a deep breath. "It's not something I enjoy talking about. But you're right. You deserve the whole story." I spend the next hour explaining about my parents and answering questions about my past and my abilities.

"Wait, you can check our phones without even touching them?" Jeremy asks, his eyes going wide.

"I can, but that doesn't mean I do. The only thing I've done is check to see where you are. Well, except for making sure you three weren't involved in the trafficking ring, and using Will's to get a link to his father. I'm sorry about that, too. I don't know how you guys could possibly forgive me for what I've done," I insist.

"I can't guarantee it's gonna be easy, but understanding why you did it helps. I'm mortified by what my father did," Luke responds.

Will stares at me for a minute. "I wasn't as close with my dad as we all were with Luke's. That doesn't mean I won't struggle sometimes with the idea that you took his life. And it's not like we're gonna tell my mom that's what happened."

"I'm not so sure she'd be too upset by it, honestly," I mutter.

"What do you mean?" he asks.

"I think she's saying your mom was one of your dad's victims," Jeremy answers for me. I nod, wishing I didn't have to share this with them.

"Wow. That's rough. I'm glad they're letting her keep her bank accounts, then. They seized his when the evidence turned up. I guess they investigated Mom and me, because they called and said that our funds wouldn't be taken." Relief washes over me. That means they weren't able to trace the money I transferred from Dave to Will and his mom. I know that I told them I wouldn't keep any more secrets, but this one will go to my grave with me.

"I'm willing to try making this work with you guys. I can't promise that I won't take other jobs. I won't promise not to hide my darkness anymore, but I will try to be more open about everything. You three are the only ones who know what I really do for a living, and you're the only ones I've ever told about my abilities. That's a level of trust that I've never had before. It's terrifying." Admitting how I feel is nearly as scary as the feelings themselves.

"But you do trust us, and that's the important part," Jeremy says, taking my hands. I let him pull me into his arms.

"I do. But what happens when the police look into these murders more? Now that you guys know, how will you be able to keep my secrets?" I can't stop myself from asking the questions, but I'm not sure I want the answers.

"The three of us have already met with the police and given our statements. We've all been cleared of any suspicion. The fact that we had no knowledge about our fathers' enterprises until the cops showed us their records helped with that." Jeremy's words echo in my head.

Will steps up beside us, wrapping his arms around me as well. "That's the only reason we gave you so much time alone. We needed to make sure they wouldn't be coming around again for anything. With us cleared, there's no reason for the police to investigate anyone connected to us further."

"You guys let me think that you never wanted to see me again because you were protecting me?" I'm shocked by Will's confession. It's more than I ever deserved; to be protected by them. And the torture was the least I could suffer for what I've done.

"Those were the hardest two days we've ever spent. There were so many moments when we wanted to call or text, or even race down here and hold you. But we had to be sure that there was nothing to connect you to the investigations," Luke explains.

I'm floored by the way these three have gone above and beyond any expectations I had. They made sure I wouldn't even be questioned by the police. Since we're involved, I'd expected to get a call and be dragged down to the precinct to answer questions at least, even if they didn't suspect me.

"I'm beginning to think you guys are as messed up as I am," I laugh.

"Maybe we are. Or maybe we're just in love with you and don't want to lose you. Either way, you're safe now." Tonight is the first time Jeremy has said anything about his feelings for me. I'm not sure how to react, even though Will has told me before that the three of them are in love with me.

"How can you be sure?" I ask.

"That we love you? That's an impossible question. But I get it; it wasn't fair for me to say it that way," Jeremy says, hugging me tighter. He eases me back to look into my eyes. "I love you, Em."

"I love you, Jer." I get a little dizzy when he spins me toward Luke. "I love you, too, Luke."

"And I've loved you for a long time, Em. I'm glad you're willing to work through this with us." He presses a kiss to my lips, gentle and chaste.

I look at Will, but he shrugs. "They already know I told you. But I'll say it again. I love you, sugarplum." My heart jumps at the pet name being used in front of the other guys.

"I love you, Will," I whisper back before he captures my lips with his for a quick kiss.

I understand this won't be easy, but I'm thrilled that they still want me. "How are we going to deal with everything, though?" I should leave it alone, but I can't.

Jeremy lets me go and paces for a minute. "I don't have to go to my father's trial. I'd rather not have people thinking I agree with the things he's done anyway."

"The trial is likely to be pretty embarrassing for your family," I say, realizing that the idea forming in my head is not a good one.

"There's nothing we can do about that," he replies, fisting his hands in his hair.

"There's nothing *you* can do about it. But there may just be something *I* can do," I offer, leaving the thought unfinished.

"Are you saying what I think you're saying?" Will sounds way too excited.

"Of course, she is," Luke answers before I have a chance. Jeremy looks at him, dumbfounded. "Em is trying to tell you that she can take him out. Then no one has to know all the sick details of the things our dads did."

It seems like both Luke and Will are all for my idea, but Jeremy covers his face with his hands. I shouldn't have offered. This is sick and twisted. I can't just kill someone to save his son from embarrassment. The idea is ridiculous. I open my mouth to apologize to Jeremy for even having the thought, but he holds up a hand and stops me.

"I want you to do it."

"What?" I ask, my jaw dropping. Even for the split second where I thought it was a good idea, I never thought he'd agree.

"You offered to kill my dad to keep his case from going to court. I want you to do it. Not for me. To protect my mom, Luke's mom, and Will's mom. There's no reason for any of them to go through that embarrassment. Make it look like he killed himself. Make him pick a fight with a guard so they kill him. I don't care. I just want this to end before anyone else gets hurt." When he's done talking, Jeremy walks over to the window and stares out into the darkness. How long have we been discussing this? Did I lay on the floor all day today?

I shake my head, already knowing the answer to both questions. "If you're sure that's what you want, I'll do it. But after, I'm going to take a break from work, and we're all going to spend some time together."

"Agreed," Jeremy says easily. Will walks over and wraps an arm around him. "We should go home so Em can take care of this."

"Before you go, I might need some help. I can't just appear there without a connection. You're going to have to go talk to your dad, so I can get in." I wince at his reaction.

"What? I don't want to talk to him."

"It's the only way she can get to him, Jer. Remember, she said that she used my phone to connect to my dad," Will explains quietly. I'm glad he listened, but at the same time, I hate that I had to do that at all. "Luke or I can go, if you don't want to," he offers.

"Shit—I can't ask you guys to do that. Okay, I'll do it. Can we do it today, or will it have to be tomorrow?" Jeremy seems anxious to get this over with. "And will you guys go with me?"

"Of course, we will, whenever we need to do," Luke insists. I'm glad that he won't have to face his father alone. Guilt ebbs at having to put him through this. At least the other two had no idea that I was targeting their fathers.

I remind myself that Jeremy made this decision on his own. It's what he wants to happen. I'm not forcing this on him. That eases some of my guilt at how much I know I'll enjoy killing this bastard. I have to figure out how to make it look like suicide, though.

"I think first thing tomorrow would be better. It'll give me a chance to work out exactly how to do it, since you want it to look like he killed himself."

Jeremy's eyes meet mine. "That part isn't too important. I doubt the life insurance will pay anyway, given what he's done and how they seized his accounts."

"Okay, but I still have to protect my secret. I can't just pop in and murder a man inside the police station without planning. I have to be careful so they don't catch me." I consider my words carefully, because I don't want to upset him any more than he already is, but I need him to understand the amount of planning that goes into these missions. "I usually have at least two days to plan a hit; ideally a week. I'm not asking for that. I just need tonight to figure it all out. Can you handle that?" I pause for a moment, then continue. "I didn't have that time to plan for Will's dad. I know that's why you caught me."

I'm not sure what I'll do if he says no. I hold my breath while he considers what I've said. Just when I think he's going to argue, he nods. "I understand. Your safety is more important than getting this done tonight. Just let me know when you're ready to go tomorrow, and we'll do it."

I release my breath, relieved that he agreed so easily. Now I just have to break into a police station filled with cops and kill a man who's locked up. Easy peasy, right? Fuck me. How do I get myself into these situations?

As soon as the guys head upstairs, I hear a knock at my door. Great, what now? I look through the peep hole, but no one is there. Opening the door, I glance up and down the hallway, but it's empty. I close the door and turn around, running right into Brynn.

"What the fuck?" I ask, shoving the fae away. "You scared me! How do you keep getting into my apartment without being seen?"

"I can't tell you that, love, or I'll have to kill you. A fae has to have some secrets, don't ya know?" they say in a sing-songy voice.

"You are the most frustrating person I've ever dealt with. What do you want?" I growl. "I have a murder to plan, and I don't need you giving me another mission right now." I shouldn't take my anger out on them, but I can't help it. I'm annoyed at the interruption.

"That's exactly why I'm here, love. We want you to take Franklin out so he has no chance of getting away. Since I heard that's what his son wants, too, I'm certain that you'll take this job," Brynn says with a smile.

"So, I can add spying on me to the list of things you've done to piss me off?" I answer, understanding that I don't have to accept or refuse the job. They know I'm going to do it regardless, so there's no reason to argue.

"If you must. Just know that we're always watching. And listening. If you ever need me, all you have to do is say my name. I'll hear you and come to help," they offer.

I laugh at the craziness of all of this. My life is comical, and there's nothing I would change about it. "After this job, I'm taking a vacation. Do you understand?"

Brynn laughs, and it's a melodic sound that reminds me of bells tinkling. "Of course, love. We'll still be watching, but you can take a trip. There's a lovely island that's secluded and would make for a wonderful sexcapade, if you're interested."

"Get out. I mean it. Go. Now. I have to plan this out, and I can't have you distracting me," I shove the fae toward the door. When they disappear in a pink cloud, I fall forward, catching myself against the door. Well, that explains how they keep getting into my apartment without being seen. I hadn't expected similar abilities to mine, but it's good to know what I'm dealing with.

WHAT'S NORMAL?

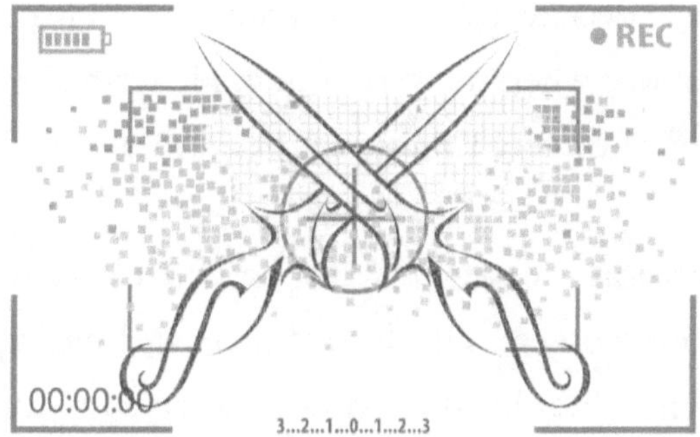

JEREMY

Back at our apartment, I start to second guess my decision. This week has been difficult for all of us. We learned that my father organized and ran a sex trafficking ring for decades, both Will's and Luke's dads were involved, and Emily killed them for it. Now I've asked the woman I'm in love with to kill my father, too.

Have I lost my mind? This is insane, right? "I'm just saying, normal people don't ask their girlfriend to kill their father.

That doesn't mean I don't want her to do it." Justifying my feelings is strange. But I'm so conflicted about all of this.

"You have to decide if this is what you want before she does it. It's not like she has the power to un-kill him. I don't think necromancy is real," Will argues.

"I mean, vampirism is real, and that's kind of the same thing," Luke jokes. I glare at them both.

"I know. My decision stands. He deserves to die for what he's done," I declare, pausing for a moment. "I just can't help thinking about when we were young. He seemed so different then. That's the man I'll mourn. Not the monster who's taken his place."

The decision is easier to stand by when I see how this is affecting our mothers. The three of them are holed up at Will's family home, since his dad's death was ruled natural causes. Even if we know the truth, there's no reason for the rest of the world to find out. The paparazzi are already camped out on the lawn, hoping to get pictures or video. It's distasteful and wrong. And I have the power to make it stop; or at least, to have Em take care of it.

"Our moms are safe for now, but we can't let them be victimized again," I say. And that's what it boils down to. I will do what it takes to protect what's left of our families.

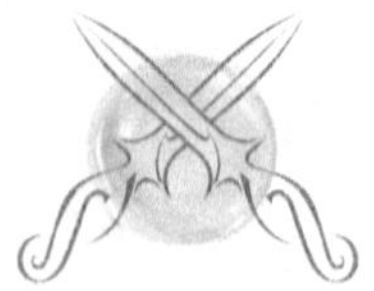

EMILY

There isn't much for me to do after the guys leave. I need to figure out the best way to dispose of Franklin. Thanks to Brynn dropping knowledge into my brain—which I may never get used to—I know the jail's schedule. The only way to get access to him is through his son, though. I don't like involving Jeremy or any of the others, but he asked me to do this.

With seized assets, there's a real chance that any of the families could lose everything. I won't let that happen. I've already set up trusts for Will and his family, so I do the same for Jeremy, then make one for Luke as well. What am I, an assassin with a soft spot? I laugh at the idea. If I'm honest with myself, I know that soft spot is what got me into this business in the first place. It's never caused me a problem before.

Until I fell for these men. I nearly gave up a job, and my life, to keep from hurting one of them. Relief washes over me, taking the feelings of guilt I've been carrying with it. I know they're not as okay with everything as they want me to believe, but I'm glad that they don't fully hate me for what I've done.

Locking myself in my secret room, I review blueprints and schematics for the jail. I go over the guards' schedules, even though they'll have very little effect on my plan.

Then I stare at the screen while I consider my options. Jer suggested making it look like suicide. I'm not sure Franklin is the suicide type. I dig into his past more and discover a connection to my own father. I've never been able to find the leader of the ring Daddy dearest worked for. Until now. Rage boils just under the surface, begging to be set free.

I'm even more invested in seeing this through. I need to take this man out. I've never tried to control someone from inside before, but I'm considering it now. If I can make him tear out his own throat with his claws, or hang himself with a bedsheet, on camera, there will be no investigation into his death. No one will bat an eye.

That idea sends me down a rabbit hole, researching wolf shifters and how their abilities work. There are tons of articles explaining the biology and magic of it. I wonder if I can pull this off.

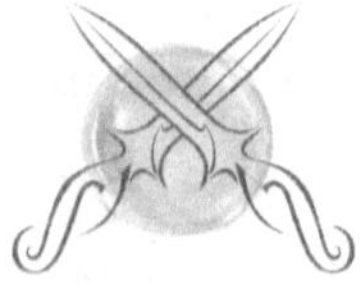

LUKE

Jer sleeps a little overnight. His decision weighs on him. I haven't said much to Em about all of this, because I'm not exactly sure what to say. I never would have imagined my dad being involved in any of this. If I hadn't seen the proof with my own eyes, I wouldn't believe it now. But even before she told us, my mom had left a message that she needed to tell me some things, and I'm certain this is what she meant.

I can't say how this new knowledge will change things, simply because I don't know yet. What I do know is that being a vampire is not easy. Dad taught me that forgiveness is key. Other supernaturals and even humans don't live nearly as long as we do. I can choose to hold a grudge and stay angry, or I can forgive and enjoy my time with Em.

There will be plenty of time later to be angry. For now, I will support and care for my friends. After checking on Jer again, I head to Will's room. He's always been an insomniac, and it's gotten worse since his father's death. I know he'd never admit it, but he's not as okay with all this as he pretends to be. I'm not saying he's mad at Em or going to do anything to hurt her. He's just conflicted, even if he doesn't see it.

I poke my head inside his room and find him fast asleep. It's the first time in months that he looks peaceful. Maybe he's not as conflicted as I thought.

Em sends us a group text, letting us know what time we need to head down to the jail. I check my watch and realize that Jer and Will still have a couple of hours to sleep before we need to get ready. I set an alarm and head back to my room, settling onto my bed with a book.

EMILY

With all my research done, I decide that a few hours of sleep are a good idea. I don't want to be groggy when I try this for the first time. Hopefully it works, otherwise, I'll have to switch to plan B. I lay in bed for a little while, staring at the ceiling. Part of me wants to send a text to my guys, but I won't interrupt their sleep, if they're actually getting some.

I drift off slowly, having time to check my alarm to be sure I'm not late. Luke was the only one to respond to the group text, so I'm hoping the other two are sleeping.

It doesn't take long for the nightmare to take hold of me, like it normally does. This time, every man I've ever killed appears. As I stab, slice, and tear at them, their faces morph into those of the men I love. In my dream, I kill Jeremy, Luke, and Will over and over. I can't stop myself from completing the missions, and I enjoy every kill. I think that's what scares me the most. I know I'm killing them, and I'm relishing it.

Can I trust myself with these men? The thought crosses my mind as I stake Luke in the heart. He dissolves in front of me, and something changes. I bolt upright in bed, tears streaming down my face. It was just a dream. None of it was real. That's a lie, and I know it. The elation I felt when I killed each man was very real, and it didn't matter to me that the men had my lovers' faces.

I truly am a monster. I don't deserve to be loved by these men. I should leave while I have the chance, before things get more complicated.

I can't do that to Jeremy, though. I promised that I would take care of his dad for him, so that all three of their moms can live in peace. I'm protecting them from the fallout that's coming. More than that, I'm selfish and want to keep the three of them for myself. I can't let my nightmares drive a wedge between us.

Knowing that any chance at sleep is gone, I get up and shower. I'll be ready early, but it's the only thing I can do right now.

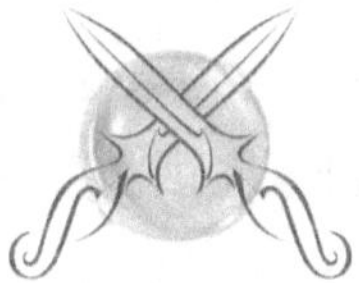

JEREMY

I can't stop the nightmares. They've been attacking me since I found out what a horrible beast my father is. I don't want the details in the media, but in my dreams, it's already there. As I walk through the streets, I see it everywhere.

Videos play on billboards, showing the depraved things my father did to women as they begged him to stop. Photos display in storefront windows, depicting the shady deals my father made. Exchanges of money, women, even drugs, are pasted up where everyone can see.

Mortification isn't even a strong enough word for what I feel at seeing these things. And somehow, every citizen I pass knows exactly who I am. Their mocking haunts me.

"Oh, there goes the Franklin boy. I wonder if he's as awful as his father."

"Look, it's the son. I bet he's gearing up to take over the old man's operation."

"You know that boy is in just as deep as his father. How could they treat women that way?"

I fist my hands in my hair and run, trying to escape it all. The voices echo in my head, accusing me of being part of it all, laying out my future, speculating at whether I'll be worse than my father in the end. I scream as I race away from them all.

As long as I've been running, I should be outside of the city, but I'm not. I stand in front of our building, staring up at the windows I know mean home. Safety calls to me, begging me to return to the people I love. I enter the building and climb the stairs quickly. With my wolf speed, it's faster than waiting for the elevator. I reach our floor quickly and dart inside the apartment.

I expect to find my chosen family waiting for me. Instead, I find their lifeless bodies, with Emily standing over them. Will's glossy eyes stare at me from beside a charred pile of ash I know has to be Luke. The wicked smile on her face terrifies me, and I have the desire to run again.

But I have nowhere else to go; nothing to live for. My life is ruined. So, I stand there, waiting for her to kill me too. Part of me welcomes it. I want to die because of how screwed up everything is now.

"Jeremy! Wake up. You're having a nightmare. Come on, man," Will's voice permeates the dream, pulling me toward consciousness.

"What happened?" I ask, opening my eyes to see Will standing over me.

"You were screaming. This nightmare was a bad one, huh? Do you wanna talk about it?" he asks, sitting beside me on the bed.

I shake my head. I can't tell him that seeing his dead body is what made me freak out like that. It's not fair to anyone for me to share that. "I'm okay. This one was just a lot. The media had everything and everyone knew who I was. They all accused me of being in on it."

"Wow, that does sound awful. It was just a dream, though. We should go ahead and get ready to leave, since we're already up. Em texted to let us know what time to get there. Luke has been dressed and waiting for hours. I don't think he slept at all." I sit up at Will's words.

"Does that mean *you* actually slept?" I know how much he's struggled with that, especially since this all started. He nods with a sad smile.

"Better than I have in years. I think it's knowing the truth that helped me with that." The quiet conviction on his face tells me that I have nothing to worry about. Emily would never hurt us. She loves us, and we love her. We're all in this together. It was just a dream.

I let a hot shower wash the remnants of the nightmare away as I prepare to see my father for the last time.

EMILY

We meet up for breakfast so that Jeremy has time to call and arrange a visit with his father. We sit in the coffee shop, drinking the delicious warm brew and munching on pastries while he makes the call.

"Yes, officer. I'd like to see my father this morning if I can." Jeremy pauses, winks at me and crinkles his nose. "Lloyd Franklin. That's right." He listens for a minute as the officer speaks. "I'm not planning to bring him anything but my disdain, sir. I just want to tell him face to face that he's no longer my father." Another short pause. "Thank you so much. I'll be right over."

I know that Jer had originally wanted the guys to go with him, but he must have changed his mind. "The guys are gonna meet us there," he says, as if reading my mind.

"Oh, okay," I respond, unsure how he knew what I was thinking.

"That officer said I can go in to see him as soon as I get there. What do you need to do to get ready?" he asks, pulling me from my thoughts.

"I just need a private spot to shift, then I'll hitch a ride in your phone. Once we're inside the precinct, I can come out. It won't matter if they make you lock it up or not. Either way, I'll be good to finish the job," I say, without realizing that I haven't told them about the guild or the assignment to kill Franklin.

"You take all of this very seriously," he replies. I nod and head toward the bathroom. I might as well see if I can shift there instead of having to go home. The bathroom is empty, so I shift, send a quick but cryptic text to let the guys know I'm going into Jer's phone, and float back to the table where I left him.

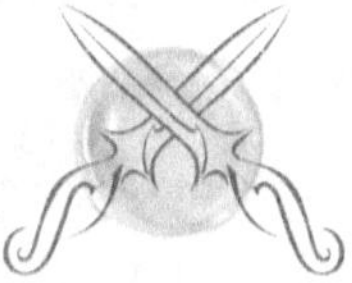

From the waiting room, Will texts Jer, and I know that's my signal to get out of the phone. I try not to think about how this entire plan makes them all accomplices. I can't afford to get distracted by the risks my guys are taking to help me with this job. I have to focus on getting this done and getting out of here.

I'm annoyed that Jeremy wants to be there when it happens. I've tried to explain to him that it's better if he doesn't see it. There's no arguing with him, though. His mind is made up, and I'm sticking to the plan.

I hang over his shoulder as we move to the interview room where he'll get to talk to his father. Of course, there will be officers in the room to ensure Jeremy's safety, and that he doesn't pass anything to the prisoner. The moment we walk into the small space, I know I have a problem.

Franklin's hands are cuffed. There's no way he's going to be able to rip out his own throat if he's chained like that. Fuck. Now what am I going to do? I spent so much time prepping this plan, and it's an amazing one if I can pull it off.

I stay in my place on Jeremy's shoulder as he takes his seat. From that vantage point, I scan the room. Two guards, one stands by the door, and the other is in position behind Franklin. Both men stand with one hand on their gun. It's an intimidating picture, and for a moment, I reconsider my plan.

I should just wait until Franklin is in his cell alone and take him out then. But I can't do that. I agreed to do this Jeremy's way, with his help. I can't change things now when I don't have the ability to explain what I'm thinking.

In my research, I read about how strong wolf shifters are, especially alphas. I wonder if I can manipulate Franklin into breaking the cuffs that hold his hands. And now I've turned my problem into a challenge. Much better.

I take a deep breath, then slide across the table. Franklin flinches when I enter him, and I push away the idea of how dirty that sounds. I've never attempted to control someone from the inside, but with all the research I've done, I think I can do it.

"Are you okay? You look annoyed," Jeremy begins the conversation that should keep his dad distracted while I work.

"Just a cold chill. What do you want?"

"Gee, Dad, aren't you glad to see your only son?" Sarcasm drips from my lover's voice, and pain stabs through my heart. I hadn't expected Franklin to be so cold and distant toward his son.

"Jeremiah, I don't have time for games. Now, either tell me why you're here, or leave so I can get back to building my defense," Franklin responds.

"Okay, then. I just wanted to tell you that we're not going to your trial. Mom and I will not support you through this. You deserve to be punished for what you've done, and I hope you get the worst possible sentence."

He pauses, and I settle into Franklin, stretching myself into the areas I need to control. I straighten his fingers, then curl them into fists. I can see through his eyes, and Jeremy's reaction tells me that his father is freaking out a little from not being in full control.

"I have one question for you, though. I know you won't answer, but I'm asking anyway. Why did you do all of this? Was it just for the money?"

I uncurl and curl Franklin's fingers again, noting that the officers on guard duty don't budge during this conversation. "You're ridiculous, son. I've done nothing wrong."

"I expected that response," Jeremy says, nodding to me. It's time. I take control of Franklin's hands, forcing them to shift into elongated claws. They almost look like his shift has gone wrong somehow. I wonder if it's because he's fighting my control.

Jeremy stands up, moving back against the wall. "What are you doing, Dad?" I'm not sure if he's feigning terror or if he's actually startled by what I'm manipulating his father into doing.

I don't think I can control his words, so I don't try to. Instead, I jerk the cuffs, snapping them in half. Then I force Franklin to stand up, facing his son. I can see his expression in the two-way mirror on the wall. He's terrified for probably the first time in his life. And the last.

Franklin fights harder against my control, and the guards pull their weapons, training them on him. "Prisoner! Sit down and put your hands on the table."

Before they can shoot or even think to taze him, I force his clawed hand up and grip his Adam's apple. The claws dig into the skin, blood pours from the wounds. I see the tears falling from Jeremy's eyes as I force Franklin to rip his own throat out. I remain standing as he falls to the floor.

Jeremy stares at the body, then looks around the room. I know he's looking for me, but I'm pixelated, so there's nothing to see. I make my way back over to his shoulder, making sure to tap him so he knows I'm there.

From here, everything goes crazy. Franklin is clearly dead, and there are three witnesses to say it was self-inflicted. Add that to the cameras that were recording the whole thing, and I should be safe. They take him to a different room and question Jeremy for two more hours before letting him go.

Will and Luke stand up as Jer enters the waiting room, with me hitching a ride. I warned them that there would be lots of questions, even if the cops watched it happen this way.

I can't help feeling guilty for putting Jer through all of this, even if it was his idea. With as smoothly as this job went, I wonder for a moment if the guys would be willing to be my team. Maybe I'll bring it up to them later.

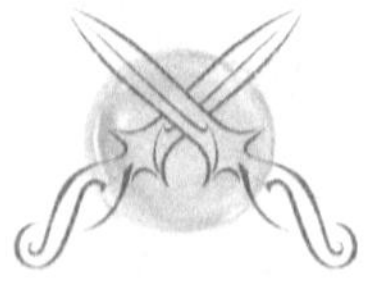

A few minutes later, we're back in the apartment ordering lunch. "Are you sure you can eat after watching all that?" Luke asks Jeremy.

"I think I'm okay. It was surreal to watch. Dad was so scared and confused. He had no idea why he did the partial shift, or why he couldn't control his hands. The whole thing was kinda like watching a B horror film."

"Cheesy and overrated?" Will offers.

I roll my eyes and smack his arm. "Stop. This isn't funny." But Jeremy and Luke are laughing at Will's joke. I have to admit, it really did play out like a weird movie. I won't tell them that, though.

"You know how I said I kill for money, right?" I figure now is as good a time as any to admit what I've already done with the money.

"Yeah, I mean, you said they were jobs. We assumed that you'd get paid for them," Luke answers.

"Well, what I didn't say before is that I got recruited by an assassin's guild, and they sent me each of your dads as a job. And, yeah, there was compensation involved." I pause and wait for a second while they process. "I did something with the money, and I need you guys to know about it."

"What did you do?" Will asks. Jeremy stares at me in disbelief.

"How could you not tell us?" he asks.

"I didn't want you to think I was only doing it because of the contract. I took your dad out because you asked me to—before the contract came through. I'm telling you about the guild and the money now, because I trust you guys. I pooled the money for all three jobs and split it between your families. There's enough money for each family to make up for what you've all lost with your fathers' crimes." I pull up the info on my phone and hand it to Will.

"That's a lot of zeros," he says, handing the phone to Luke.

"Holy shit," Luke exclaims, passing it to Jeremy.

"Is this the total? Or is this what each family got?" Jer asks.

"That's what each family got. Your moms will be taken care of and there will be a lot of money left for you guys. I hope that's okay." I start to panic, thinking that they'll get angry that I've given their families blood money.

Will drags me into his arms. "That is a very generous thing to do, especially when that was your payment for doing a job."

"I can't believe you did this. Mom can get the house back now. Thank you," Luke says quietly.

Jeremy just looks at me. "I don't know what to say," he whispers.

"Look, you guys don't have to say anything. I didn't do it so you'd thank me. I did it because it felt like the right thing to do. Given everything your moms and families have been through, they deserve to be taken care of. I want them to have this money. And it can't be traced to me at all, so no one will ever know where it came from. It'll look like your moms were hiding money from your dads, and the cops will let it go." I buried my tracks very carefully to ensure that the police would not be able to confiscate this money or seize it in any way.

"Now that all of this is behind us, we should really talk about that vacation you mentioned," Luke says.

"Oh, you remember that, do you?" I tease.

"We all do. And we're hoping you wanna go somewhere sunny and warm," Will says.

"Why's that?" I ask, curious at their reasoning.

"So, we can see you lounging around in a bikini when we have to leave the room, and nothing at all the rest of the time," Jeremy answers.

My cheeks turn red, and I dip my head to avoid their eyes. These three are a handful, but they're mine. "Tropical vacation it is, then. Have you guys looked into any resorts or cruises?"

"There are a lot of options," Luke says, pulling up some info on his phone.

A poof of pink in the corner reminds me of what Brynn said yesterday. "I actually have a line on a deserted island, if you're interested," I admit. "My boss said that the guild has one."

I can tell from their reaction that the guys are intrigued by the idea.

EPILOGUE

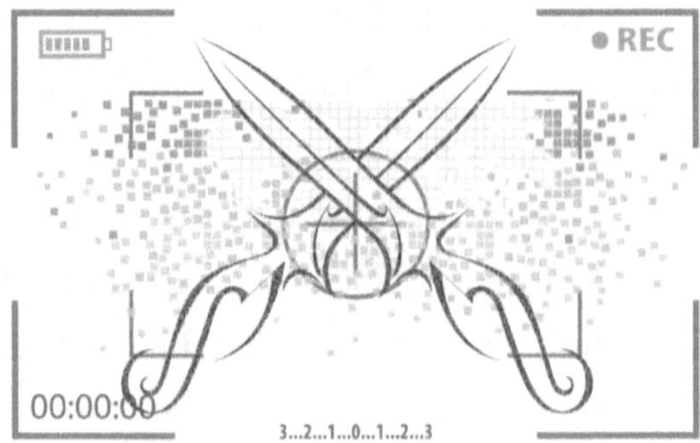

SIX MONTHS LATER

EMILY

"I don't want to go back, either, but you promised your mom we'd all come to dinner," I say, throwing my towel at Luke.

"That shouldn't count. It was forever ago, before I knew we'd be traveling for six months," he argues.

Will steps between us, pulling me to him and kissing me deeply. "You two need to stop arguing about this and start packing. Our flight leaves soon." And just like that, he releases me and walks off.

I go back to tossing clothes into my suitcase. What was I thinking buying new clothes while we've been away? I'll never get them all into this suitcase. A moment later, Jeremy walks in carrying a large suitcase I've never seen before.

"You're gonna need this," he says, laying it on the bed and unzipping it. Then the fucker walks away laughing.

"I can't believe none of you are going to help me pack!" I yell at them, before collapsing into a fit of giggles at how absolutely normal things have been for us the last six months. I mean, I never expected our beach trip to become semi-permanent, but we all love it here.

In fact, I've already put a sizeable down payment on our condo and signed a purchase agreement without even telling the guys. Which means, I really don't have to pack all of this. I smack myself in the forehead and start putting clothes away, sorting what I really need and leaving what won't be useful. Even if this is just our vacation home, the outfits I'm leaving will be more useful here.

I zip my suitcase and carry it to the front door. Three sets of eyes lock onto me, realizing that I'm not taking everything. I play innocent for a moment. "What? I'm ready to go now."

"Where are all your clothes?" Luke asks, giving me a curious look.

"Well, most of them are in my dresser, in our condo," I smirk.

Will laughs. "You bought the condo? That's hilarious." He turns to Jeremy and holds out his hand. "You owe me twenty bucks." Then Luke. "And you owe me fifty."

"You guys bet on if I'd buy the condo or not?" I'm amused and floored by how well Will knows me, and how easily he can con the other two.

Tucking the money in his wallet, he strolls over to me and kisses me again. "Thanks for being reliable, sugarplum." Before I can respond, he grabs my suitcase and heads out the door.

"It's not like we can't afford it," I say, trying to justify the purchase. "And your moms can all use it when we're not. It'll be like a time share, but we actually own it."

Jeremy pats me on the head on his way out the door. "Whatever you say, Em."

I turn to Luke. "Is he really mad about it?"

Luke shakes his head. "No. He actually bet that you'd tell us you bought it after the first month we were here. Will was the one who said you'd slip up today and tell us that you did it. I thought you'd hold out until we got home to admit it."

"So, you all knew that I was going to? Damn. It was supposed to be a surprise." Disappointment crosses my features, and Luke pulls me into his arms. I can't help smiling at him as he kisses me deeply. The past six months have been the best of my life. I don't want this to end.

Logically, I know heading home doesn't mean things will change. And we are going to have to put my apartment on the market if we plan to get a bigger place in the city or near it. So, we have to go back. At least to settle things and get our living arrangements sorted.

"Mom said she has a surprise for us. She's not sure how you'll feel about it, though. But I couldn't get her to tell me anything else," Luke says as he breaks our kiss.

"Come on, guys, we need to go," Will calls. Luke and I race down the path to the car.

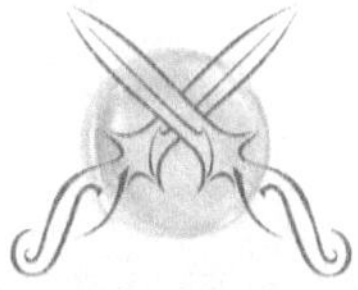

A few hours later, we sit in the formal living room at Luke's family home. It's a gorgeous house, and his mom has made quite a few changes since we've been gone. Most of the fancy artwork is gone, along with the stuffy furniture.

"Wow, Ms. Donovan, I love what you've done with the place," I say as she pours us tea.

"Now, dear, I've asked you to call me Kate. Please. Or Mom. I'm okay with either," she insists.

"I'm sorry, Kate. It's just hard to break old habits," I answer.

"Can you tell us the big news, Mom? It's making me crazy," Luke says, fidgeting in his seat next to me.

"Lucas! Don't rush me. I'm getting to it." Kate pauses and looks around the room. "I'm glad you like the changes, Emily. Because I'd like to sign the house over to the four of you."

My jaw drops. Luke nearly chokes on his tea. Jeremy's eyes go wide, and Will is the only one able to respond. "We'd love that, Kate. Thank you."

"But, it's your home," I argue.

She shakes her head. "No, dear. It was *his* home. This house never felt like a home to me. I'll be much happier with the new place I just bought. After all, you did give each of us a rather nice nest egg, didn't you?"

I can't cover the look of shock on my face. No one is supposed to know that I'm the one who provided that money. How did she find out?

"Now, don't freak out, dear. Carol, Jean, and I know that you took care of our problems for us. We also know about the money. And no, our sons did not tell us. We figured it out from how protective and nurturing you are. I, for one, am excited to have an assassin in the family. You never know when you'll need that kind of help." Kate grins at me, and I know I have nothing to fear with her knowing my secret. I've been family to her since her husband died—okay, since I killed him.

"I don't know what to say. So, I'll say thank you. For the house and for keeping my secret. I really appreciate it, especially since I'm the one who messed up your lives so much," I offer.

Kate shakes her head and reaches for my hand. "Emily, dear. You did not mess up our lives. You saved us. The boys had no idea what their fathers were like behind closed doors, which was intentional. We never intended for them to find out. But you figured out our secrets and saved us from them. Then you made sure we had what we needed financially. That's not messing anything up. That's taking care of family."

I let her pull me off the couch and into a big hug. "I'll be leaving after dinner, so you kids can move in tonight if you want." Kate releases me and strolls off toward the kitchen.

"How do you guys feel about this?" I ask. I don't want to be too excited if this isn't something that they want.

"Anything that makes you happy is what we want," Luke says.

"It won't feel weird living in the house where your dad died?" I'm not trying to talk him out of it, but I don't want him to be stuck, either.

He grabs my hands and drags me down onto his lap on the couch. "I understand that you're worried. It's okay. I grew up in this house. This will always feel like home to me, especially with the three of you here. So, unless *you* don't want to move in here, let's just be happy that we now own a house that we didn't exactly have to pay for."

Will laughs, "She kinda already paid for it, though, didn't she?"

Jeremy punches his arm and shakes his head. "That's not what he meant, and you know it. We should go back to the apartments and pack up before time to be back for dinner. Then we can get everything moved tonight."

"Do you think the landlord will be angry that we're moving out so quickly without notice?" I ask, considering making the offer to pay for another month or two of both apartments to smooth things over.

"We'll only be moving out two months early. I already called him when you finally told us you bought the condo. Henry is fine with us moving. He's already got two different couples interested. The way I see it, this makes things easier on him." Jeremy's explanation makes sense, but also surprises me. I had no idea he'd called our landlord about this.

"How did you know we'd be moving?" I press.

Will takes my hand, drawing my attention away from Jeremy. "Because we started looking for houses outside of the city a couple of weeks after we left for vacation. You need more privacy for your work—both jobs, and we need more space for all of us. We were gonna surprise you, but you beat us to it."

I feel bad for ruining their surprise, but I'm glad we can settle into Luke's family home. I love the idea of making this enormous house our own. And I'm pretty sure there are enough bedrooms and office spaces that I can have an even better set up than I do at the apartment.

"How are we going to get everything packed and loaded up before dinner?" I ask, suddenly on board for the idea. The sooner we get settled, the better.

"Well, one of the companies my family owns is a moving company. As soon as Kate told us, I sent a text, and the truck is on its way. They'll have boxes and packing material for us, and will help pack if we want," Will explains with a smirk.

"We need to get moving, then," I insist, jumping from Luke's lap and dashing into the kitchen to let Kate know about our plans.

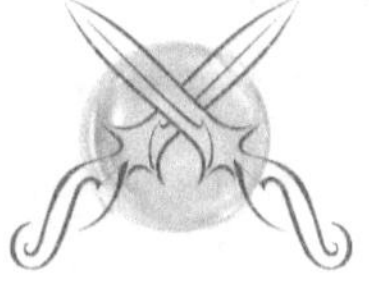

The moving crew is awesome. The guys give them carte blanche to pack their entire apartment, leaving Jeremy, Will, and Luke free to help me pack my stuff. I'm glad they understand that I like to keep my equipment private. I let Jeremy and Luke pack up my costumes and wigs, while Will and I pack the secret room.

"You have so much computer equipment. This is some amazing stuff. Do we need to figure out which room to set it up in tonight? Or do you still have some vacation left?" He's teasing, I know, but it's still cute.

"I think it can wait until tomorrow. I'll have to plug the laptop in just in case there's an urgent message, but jobs come through a different way, so that's not an issue." I realize that I never told them much about the guild or how I get assignments from them. That'll be a conversation for later, then.

No more secrets between us, ever. I will tell these men everything, no matter how big or small. We'll figure it all out together, one step at a time.

Once we have both apartments packed up and loaded onto the truck, we head back home. Home. That's always been such a foreign word to me, until I met these guys. I feel like I've been home ever since we started dating, and now that we're moving into a house that we own together, it feels even more right.

I know I'll have to get back to work soon, with my cam job and assassinations. I can't put it off forever. Brynn has been way too understanding about all the jobs I've turned down the past six months.

We pull into the driveway and start unloading everything. Luke instructs the movers where to stack boxes so they're out of the way and we can start organizing tomorrow.

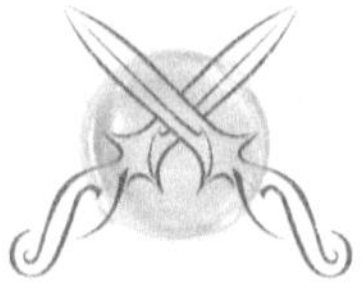

ONE YEAR LATER
EMILY

The past year and a half has been crazy. Somehow killing three men brought me closer to their sons. We split our time between the condo on the beach and the house outside the city. My guys helped me set up an office and cam room in each. I have twice as many wardrobe and wig choices between the two houses.

It should feel weird that they help me with my jobs now, but it doesn't. They've taken to their new roles as my team in the best ways possible. The tiny pink orbs continue to find me, no matter which home we're at. Or Brynn shows up unannounced. I'm not a fan of him spying on me, but I understand.

I consider everything we've been through as I finish a private call with my next mark. Mr. Day is a freak for sure, and he's trying to reconnect Franklin's circle that I disbanded. I won't let that happen. "Same time next week?" I ask with a soft smile.

"You mean our time is already up?" He pretends to be clueless, but I refuse to let him push me.

"It is. And I do have other clients, so I have to go. I'll see you soon." Sooner than you think, even. He begrudgingly agrees and I disconnect the call.

"I hate watching you on these calls. Just thinking about those pervs wanting to touch you makes me want to eat their faces," Jeremy growls.

"I know, and that's why you're not supposed to be in here while I'm on the private calls," I scold him, then focus on his expression. He's upset about something that has nothing to do with my camming. "What's up?"

"We're gonna have to head back to the city earlier than planned," he says, holding up a pink orb.

"They're giving you my assignments now?" I ask, letting him place the orb in my hand. Interesting. "Who is this?" I ask the orb as if it can speak back to me. Of course Jer thinks I'm talking to him.

"I don't know," he says "you're the only one who can get the info, remember? You have to take the job so we can find out."

I shake my head and lock eyes with him. "No. I'm not quite ready to go back to work just yet." As soon as I say the words, the orb disappears.

Jeremy shrugs and walks away. I shower, washing off the makeup and glitter I use while camming, slip into a bikini, then stroll out the sliding door to the beach. This place is paradise, and I intend to enjoy it, even if it means turning down a job or two.

I stare at the water, allowing myself to wonder if I made the right decision about that last offer, when a pair of strong arms wrap around me from behind. I freeze for a moment, taking a deep breath of his scent. A smile tilts my lips and I spin in Will's arms.

Our lips meet in a feverish kiss, feral and desperate. He lifts me, and I wrap my legs around his waist as he carries me back to our condo. As much as I'm into voyeurism, I don't want our neighbors to see us fucking on the beach. Plus, sand is abrasive and uncomfortable when it gets involved.

Once we're back inside, Luke takes me from Will and carries me upstairs to our bedroom. It's spacious, and the balcony doors are open, letting the thin curtains dance in the breeze. Two of my men lay me down on the bed, their hands exploring my body in ways that make me ache for more.

I want them but can't stop thinking about pissing Jeremy off. "What's wrong, sugarplum?" Will asks, both of them pausing to stare at me.

"You fought with Jer, didn't you?" Luke asks.

"How did you know?" My eyes go wide and I stare back at him.

"He's in the basement sulking," he responds. "You should get him to come up here." At Luke's words, Will holds up his cell phone, and they both grin.

"I'll be right back," I say, shifting into pixels and diving into Will's phone. I find my way to Jeremy quickly. For a moment,

I feel like I'm spying on him. But that's not what this is about, and I have to remind myself of that.

I shift back, standing behind him. "Still mad?" He jumps at my voice, then turns to face me.

"Maybe. I just think you should have taken that job," he argues.

I step closer to him, running my hands up his stomach and chest. "But then I wouldn't be able to do this, because I'd be working." I tease my fingers into his hair, pulling him down to me for a kiss. My tongue tangles with his, and he finally relents, wrapping his arms around me and deepening the kiss.

"This is better," he admits, scooping me up and racing up the stairs to the bedroom. He doesn't even look shocked to find Luke and Will already there, waiting for us.

The three of them exchange a glance, then Jeremy tosses me at the bed. I'm caught off guard as I bounce on the soft mattress before Will grabs my arm and straps me to the headboard. "You know this won't hold me," I threaten with a smirk.

"We just wanna see how long you'll let us play," Luke answers.

Fuck, it gets me hot when they work together like this. I might actually let them take the lead this time. It's hard for me to give up control, and they know it. But we're working on it with small trust exercises like this one. I know I can escape any time, and they get to see what I'll let them do to me. My bikini bottoms are soaked at the idea of what's coming.

Jeremy drags my bottoms off before looping restraints around my ankles, spreading me open for them. For a moment, I have to remind myself to breathe. I don't want a panic attack to ruin what we've got going here. And I can get free at any time. These three won't hurt me.

Luke unties my bikini top and slowly pulls the strip of fabric away, letting the straps tease my nipples to peaks. I'm already worked up to the point of feeling desperate for them. I don't know how much more I can take.

Will shifts his index finger into a feather, and I know I'm not going to last. The soft, nearly tickling sensations that rock my body as he trails it along my skin make me buck and writhe. "Now, sugarplum, you have to be a good girl to get what you want. Understand?"

"Please, Will. I need it." Fuck, I'm already begging, and they just got started. This has to be a new record.

"Soon, kitten. Just relax and let us worship you," Luke insists, trailing his fangs along my neck and chest, before biting down on the side of my breast. He's been finding new and interesting places to bite me, just to see what happens.

I feel a gush of moisture from my core, and Jeremy hums his approval. "That's what I like to see. Now I'm going to taste you, and you're going to scream my name when you come. Then the three of us are going to fuck you until you can't think straight."

Before I can respond, Jeremy is between my legs, lapping at my pussy. He licks and sucks until I don't think I can take any more, but I refuse cry out. I want to see how much more I can take too. While he continues, Luke gently bites my nipples and breasts. Will continues his torturous feather trail down my body.

I can't hold back the orgasm any longer, so I cry out. "Jeremy!" The moment his name is off my lips, they all stop. "Wait, why are you stopping?" I look from one to another, but they just stare at me. "Please, I need you all. Fuck me already," I beg.

That gets them moving, changing position and adjusting my restraints. It doesn't take long to figure out what they're doing, because it's easier for me to take all three of them if they turn me on my side. Will's cock slides along my entrance, rubbing against my clit and making me squirm again.

Luke's fingers spread lube along my rosebud as he preps me, dipping one finger inside, then another to stretch me for his dick. While they tease me toward another release, Jeremy positions himself next to my head, where I can see his cock. I lick my lips and he eases it into my mouth, giving me what I want.

Luke enters me first, sliding his dick into me slowly, allowing time for me to stretch and relax. Once he's fully seated, he pulls back a little to give Will room to enter. Will's cock pushes into me at a teasing pace. I want to buck my hips and make them move, but I can't. I'm pinned between the three men, and I have no choice but to let them control our pace.

I groan around Jeremy's dick as Will and Luke finally start to move, thrusting in and pulling out of me in tandem. Each thrust shoves Jeremy's cock further down my throat and I have to swallow to keep it from choking me. I try to focus on sucking him off, but all I can do is relax and let him fuck my throat while the other two fill me.

The three of them pick up the pace, finally finding a punishing rhythm that sends me over the edge way too soon. I can't cry out with my release, so I hum instead. The vibration sets Jeremy off and he shoots streams of cum down my throat before pulling out and letting me lick him clean.

"That's it. That's my good girl. Clean it all up," he says quietly.

Luke and Will switch to sliding out and thrusting in opposite each other, since Jeremy is no longer in my mouth. Each thrust pushes me closer to another orgasm, and I'm not sure how many more I can take. They thrust over and over, picking up speed and pounding harder into me. I'm getting close when Jeremy slips his hand down my stomach to tease my clit.

That sensation is all it takes to completely undo me. I scream with my release, clenching down on them and milking theirs out as well. I collapse on the bed when they pull out of me, not noticing that the restraints are gone.

Jeremy cleans me up with a warm cloth while the other two take care of themselves. I want to offer to help them, but I'm sated and can't move. "Just rest, love. We have all the time in the world here," Jeremy tells me as I drift off to sleep.

I wake a few hours later, noticing that the sun is lower in the sky. Stretching, I find myself alone and still naked. I take a quick shower and slip into another bikini because it's still scorching here, even in the afternoon.

Walking down the stairs slowly, I hear voices in the kitchen. I slow down and listen as I approach. "When do you want to do it?" Luke asks.

"As soon as she wakes up," Jeremy responds.

Curiosity grips me and I walk into the kitchen. "What are you two plotting?"

Their eyes go wide, and they exchange a look. "Nothing," they say in unison. Now I know they're lying.

I glare at them for a moment. Something catches my eye, and I turn to see Will kneeling beside me. Jeremy and Luke join him. Each of them pulls a ring box from their pockets.

"We can't exactly make this legally binding, but we'd love it if you'd marry us," Luke says.

"Em, we love you, and want to spend our lives with you," Jeremy adds.

"Please, sugarplum?" Will asks.

"How could I say no to a proposal like that?" I ask, touching each man's cheek. "Yes, of course. We can have a small ceremony here on the island." I smile as they place the rings on my finger, and I see how they fit together, forming a flower. This is our beginning, and nothing can stop us now.

The Series Continues...

Follow **The Cursed Blade** organization as it recruits new members, and watch assassins fall in love...continuing in Book 2 – **Elemental Blade**.

I'm being hunted, and I have nowhere to hide.

As if being an elemental witch living in the heart of the city isn't enough of a struggle, I find myself on the run from someone who wants to use my powers for their own benefit.

Alone and terrified, I'm discovered by three handsome strangers. I have no choice but to trust them with my life while they hide me away from the threats against me.

These men see something in me that I can't find in myself. They push me to train, crafting me into a weapon.

With them by my side, I face the biggest challenge of my life. There is only one goal: survive.

About the Author

M.P. Starkweather is a wife, mother, author, poet, casual online gamer, self-proclaimed fan-girl, and full-time nerd. She writes free-form poetry, paranormal romance, sci-fi romance, reverse harem romance, omegaverse romance, and is branching out into contemporary romance. In her free time, she enjoys writing, reading, Dungeons & Dragons, table top games with her husband and friends, and playing with her son. M.P. also enjoys tv, movies, and music across various genres.

To get the most up-to-date information about her latest releases and book signings, check out www.mpstarkweather. com or follow her on your favorite social media site.

Also by M.P. Starkweather

Standalones – Contemporary RH

Finding Fiona
Standalones - Contemporary RH OV

Forsaken Omega – free with newsletter signup

Cold Princes

Knot My Valentine
The Pack Next Door – Contemporary RH OV series

Princess or Knot

Fiancée or Knot

<u>Queen or Knot</u>

<u>The Pack Next Door: The Original Trilogy</u>

<u>Christmas or Knot</u>
Standalones – Paranormal RH

<u>The Wayward Girl</u>
The Cursed Blade Series – Paranormal w/ different pairings

<u>Digital Blade</u> – RH
<u>Elemental Blade</u> – RH
Vampires at Midnight - Paranormal RH series
<u>Blood Moon</u>

<u>Blood Lost</u>

<u>Blood War</u>

<u>Vampires at Midnight: The Complete Trilogy</u>
VaM/HoF Crossover Novella - Paranormal RH

<u>Blood Wolf</u>— free with newsletter signup
Hunters of the Forest - Paranormal RH series

<u>Wolf Bane</u>

<u>Wolf Caged</u>

<u>Wolf Moon</u>

<u>Hunters of the Forest: The Complete Trilogy</u>
Forged by Magic - Sci-fi/Fantasy M/F series

<u>Hidden</u>

<u>Betrayed</u>

<u>Saved</u>

<u>Forged by Magic: The Complete Trilogy</u>
Daydreams and Sunsets - a collection of poetry

<u>Daydreams and Sunsets</u>